The Perfect Wedding Day...

Disaster

a novella

Stephen M. Goodrum

Stephen M. Goodrum

ISBN-13: 978-0615658322 (SMGoodrum,plc)

ISBN-10: 0615658326

Dedication

My farmer's daughter bride of forty years,
Donna Lesher Goodrum

And in memory of Reverend Ron J. Heilner
December 8, 1946 - March 9, 2011

Stephen M. Goodrum

$\mathscr{Preface}$

All of the incidents depicted in this fictional story are inspired by true events that were either experienced by myself or by my wife, Rev. Donna Goodrum, or witnessed by other ministers and wedding attendants. The actual disaster in the first section is completely fictional and there is no First Presbyterian Church in Bloomfield Hills. Have fun!

~~ Rev. Stephen M. Goodrum, M.Div.,M.A.

Stephen M. Goodrum

Table of Contents

The Prelude

Katherine Hatfield straightened her veil and wiped the tears from her cheeks on this, her wedding day, the third Saturday in August. She turned to her fiancé, Alexander Burgess, and gave him her best smile as her maid of honor arranged her long white flower laced wedding gown. She had dreamed of this day for so many years, she couldn't believe it was finally here. She couldn't believe it had turned out quite like this. She'd known she would shed tears at this beautiful moment in her life, but she didn't think it would be from laughing so hard that her cheeks hurt and her belly ached. It had all started forty-eight hours earlier.

Stephen M. Goodrum

The Rehearsal

Stephen M. Goodrum

Chapter One

The church was set back from the street by a lush green manicured lawn with a fountain surrounded by a flower garden at its center. The tree lined circular drive brought you to the trademark gothic stone edifice of the First Presbyterian Church. It was the postcard perfect place for a never to be forgotten, elegant wedding.

The stretch limo carrying Katherine and her four attendants on this beautiful Thursday summer evening pulled up under the portico and stopped. Alexander Burgess, her fiancé, opened her door and a warm breeze touched her hair with the scent of gardenias. Alexander took her hand, helped her out of the car and gave her a modest kiss on the cheek.

"Welcome to your rehearsal, Katie," he said with a smile.

"You mean, *our* rehearsal, Alex dear," she replied, thinking, *you mean your mother's rehearsal*.

The Burgess and Hatfield family's limos followed extending around the drive and out onto the Woodward

Avenue in Bloomfield Hills, one of the wealthiest communities in Michigan.

Alex stood in the doorway, welcoming everyone into the narthex of the church. He waited until all of the attendants, parents, siblings, spouses, friends and children were inside and the outer doors were closed. He waited a few minutes more until everyone's eyes had adjusted to the darker interior light before opening the doors to the nave of the sanctuary just as his mother, Mrs. Beatrice Burgess, had instructed. Katherine knew that this theatrical entrance to the historical church was all to leave her family from Norvell Township speechless. That just proved how little her future mother-in-law knew about her family and friends.

Alex and his best man pulled open the huge solid oak doors and ushered everyone into the back of the two thousand seat, polished wood and stained glass sanctuary. The damp smell of stone, Old English polish and candle wax surrounded them

Katherine's Dad exclaimed: "Ho-lee sheei...

"Sssh now, Pop," Katherine's mother, Karen Hatfield, interrupted.

A gasp came from Alex's mother as Katherine's family snickered.

"This is a place of reverence," Katherine's mother continued. Looking over to the Burgess family she said, "He's lost a lot of his hearin' with runnin' tractors and combines, and talkin' all hours of the night on that noisy CB radio. Ain't that right, Pop?"

He nodded. "Uh, sorry, Missus Burgess, and Mister Burgess. It sure is a be-yewtiful church."

Katherine just shook her head and dared not look at her sisters who were ready to burst out laughing. She looked over at Alex and saw he was hiding a grin on his face along with his groomsmen, two who were doubled over by one of the pews. Looking closer, she saw it was her two brothers. She gave them the evil eye and they promptly straightened up.

"Welcome everyone, to the First, Presbyterian, Church," echoed a booming bass voice from down the aisle at the front of the sanctuary. The Reverend Dr. Phillip Stewart, Ph.D., motioned everyone down the carpeted aisle to the railing and steps that led up to the chancel and altar.

Looking across the front, they could see the choir loft and the four rank organ keyboards with pipes extending from floor to ceiling. Taking up the entire center was a monolithic wood carved altar with more organ pipes and intricate carved wood behind it reaching to a circular window of stained glass depicting the risen Christ ascending or descending from heaven, depending on your point of view. To the right side of sanctuary stood a six foot tall white marble statue of Jesus holding a shepherds staff in one hand and a lamb in the other with several small sheep at his feet, the designated spot for the children's message. On the left side stood an imposing elevated stone pulpit where the pastor climbed a flight of circular stairs to reach the pinnacle and proclaim God's word from on high to the adults. Those in the pews just in front of the pulpit would have to look straight up to be attentive. No doubt Sunday late comers were ushered to these empty seats.

Pastor Stewart gathered everyone around him in a semi-circle, waiting for all conversations to stop in a solemn and uncomfortable silence.

"Thank you. Let me begin by saying that all of us here at Furst Prez-b'terian are honored to have the celebration of marriage for the Alexander Burgess family and the beautiful Katherine Hatfield and her family.

"Now, a few rules. No photography. No cell phones. Both will be checked by the church ushers at the door. This is a sacred occasion and we should not have it marred by unsightly flashes or interrupted by ring tones, buzzes, or pop songs. No sandals, running shoes, sports or casual wear." The pastor paused and he looked at Katherine's father who was wearing a bright blue Hawaiian shirt with a golden sun setting behind green palm trees and bright red flowers.

"Also, no elaborate displays of affection." He looked over his glasses at Katherine and Alexander. They dutifully nodded at him. "We are Prez-b'terians. We do everything decently and in order."

One of the groomsmen, Alexander's brother, whispered "God's frozen people," and those around him snickered. Pastor Stewart ignored them.

"Now, I will direct the wedding party where to stand and where to walk, and for the couple, when to talk. And, please turn off, not down. Yes, turn off, your cell phones right now. Again, this is a place of reverence and I do not want us to be interrupted during the rehearsal."

17

Everyone dutifully reached into their pockets and purses and turned off their assortment of phones and portable devices. The pastor looked over to Katherine's father who had stood still during the commotion. He saw the pastors look, smiled and shook his head. He pulled out the lining of his empty pockets and said. "Got no cell phone, Rev-rend."

Once everyone had returned to attention, Pastor Stewart began pointing at the attendants. "Bridesmaids, to your left. Groomsmen to your right. Parents in the front pews. Children with their parents And the happy couple stand before me. I'll wait."

Beatrice, Alexander's mother, quietly walked up to the pastor extending her hand and humbly thanking him for officiating her son's wedding. The pastor said she was most welcomed and motioned her to her place at the end of the first pew next to her husband, Mr. Eugene Burgess, President and CEO of Burgess Financial Group and current president of the First Church's Board of Elders. The pastor then drew Alexander and Katherine together in front of him. He instructed them that they were to stand two to three feet apart during the ceremony, giving the congregation a view of the one conducting the service. He would also be standing two steps higher than the couple during the nuptials, symbolizing in his mind God's presence and blessing on them and their marriage. He told them they were only to touch when putting on the rings and giving each other a chaste kiss following the pronouncement. He said this in such a way to emphasize that this was a serious matter. Just then laughter erupted from the bridesmaids.

"Please, ladies. This is a house of worship." He glared at them and the women promptly went quiet and stood at attention. He turned to the groomsmen for any bad behavior but they were standing with their heads down and turned away from him.

"Alright, I will now talk through the ceremony with the couple." He then parted them the required two feet between their shoulders. "I'll give my introduction with everyone standing, then I'll ask your father..." He paused and looked at Katherine's father with a look of irritation at the thought of asking this country bumpkin to say anything in public, especially in his sanctuary. Mr. Hatfield smiled and gave him a little wave. "Then you two will stand facing me as you are now and I will begin the liturgy from the Book of Common Prayer."

"After the liturgy, I will ask both of your intentions to be married, in which you will both say *I Will*, not the common *I Do*. Love is a matter of the will, free will, I might add, that is, tempered by Calvin's concept of providence. This will all be a part of my sermon which, after your 'I wills,' I will ascend to the pulpit and give a short dissertation on love, not the emotional notion of romantic love, but the theological perspective of our will submitting to God's will."

Just then a loud ringing of what sounded like an old desk phone filled the chancel. The pastor looked around the wedding party and then at Katherine's father for the culprit. Everyone was turning their heads and looking back and forth hoping that whoever had not turned off their phone and interrupted the pastor would hurry and turn the offensive ringing off. By the third ring, the pastor looked down at his pants, reached into the pocket and retrieved his phone. He quickly answered it, told them he would call back and hung up. He acted as if nothing had happened.

"Alright, I will then come down and stand before you as you state your vows repeated after me, then, exchange rings, again repeating after me. You will then go up to the altar, light your unity candle and walk down to the edge of the steps here where you will kneel and wait for the benediction. After my blessing, I will have you stand and I will pronounce you husband and wife. And remember, just a modest kiss on the lips. No smashing mouths together. It should be done decently and in order. I will now have my assistant, Reverend Eunice Middleton come out and pace you through the choreography of the ceremony." He turned to the side of the chancel and called out, "Yuu-nis?"

A smiling middle-aged woman walked out from the choir loft to greet the wedding party. "So good to have all of you here this evening," she said as she passed the Pastor who was walking out of the chancel. Once he was out of sight, Eunice smiled and hugged the couple, then stepped down to shake hands with every member of the bridal party and the family, giving the ring bearer and the flower girls a pat on the head. She gave the Burgess family a polite handshake. She gave the Hatfields her hand to shake, but they gave her a big hug. She returned to the front and began guiding them through the sequence of the wedding service. A half hour later, they were back in the limos for a one mile drive to the members-only Bloomfield Hills Country Club.

Chapter Two

The wedding party enjoyed a formal six course dinner of filet mignon, lake trout and ocean crab legs in the Sunroom of the Bloomfield Hills Country Club. Established by wealthy Detroit industrialists in the lake strewn country fields twenty miles northwest of the city in1912, its "*purpose shall be to promote Social Intercourse, Golf and Automobiling.*"

After dessert, the bridal party reviewed their respective plans for Friday's bachelor and bachelorette parties. The boys were starting with a couple of rounds of golf, followed by a cookout and drinks on the deck of the Country Club, dinner jacket required, with a poker game to follow. The girls were going out for a day of shopping at Somerset Collection and dinner at J. Alexander's nearby, followed by a slumber party at the Burgess mansion, discreet sleep wear expected.

These final two days before the wedding had been well planned and orchestrated by the bride and the

Burgess family. This was to be one of Bloomfield's most talked about society weddings of the season.

Before parting ways, Katherine grabbed Alex's hand and pulled him into a small lounge off the dining room. She gave the room a once over and saw no one there to interrupt their private minute together. She drew him close and he put his arms around her

"Zander, I'm so happy. I can't wait to become your wife and spend the rest of my life with you."

"I love you too, Katie." He pressed his lips to hers.

She felt his tongue slip into her mouth, and she met it with hers. They pressed themselves to each other as close as clothes would allow. When she felt his hand come around her ribs, she grabbed it and pressed it against her breast. She let out a small whimper and he groaned with longing. When their mouths parted, Alex dipped his head to the crook of her neck and nibbled. A shiver ran down her spine. As her hand reached for his rear end, they heard a knock at the door. They quickly parted and she straightened up her clothes.

"You kids in here?" boomed Alex's father.

"Yes, Dad. We're over here just saying goodbye before we head our separate ways."

"Okay. Sorry to interrupt. Your Mom and I are heading out. We'll see you at the house when you get home. Mom wants to go over the seating arrangement one more time."

"Great. See you soon, Dad."

After Mr. Burgess left and closed the door, Katherine turned toward Alex and put her arms back around his neck. "Talk about *inter-rupture,* you okay down there?"

"No, but I guess I'll have to be, at least for the next couple of nights."

"Poor baby." She took his hand, raised the palm to her lips and kissed it. "That's from me to you, if you need it."

"I'm saving myself for you, my beautiful bride-to-be."

"And I'll have a surprise for you under my wedding gown, Zander Pander. But no lookie nookie till we're married."

"I can't wait to see you coming down the aisle."

"I'll be coming for you, hubby-bubby. Then we'll dine and dance and party. Then you can come for me," she said with a wink.

"Oh, Baby!"

Katherine kissed him quick, grabbed his hand. "We better go."

"Yeah, going home without you. And even worse, going over a seating chart, again, with my mom. Good God, I can't wait till Saturday when all of this planning will be over."

"Then it'll be our day. Our Perfect Wedding Day," Katherine said. "And then our perfect wedding night. Til then, be a good boy."

"Yes, dear."

~~~

It was a bright and beautiful Friday morning, June 13th. The groomsmen were out on the golf course by eight a.m. hoping to get a couple of rounds in before the afternoon heat, and it was supposed to be a hot one. The jet stream had bulged northward up into the U. P. of Michigan and Canada, making for one of the hottest days of the year. The forecast called for temperatures in the nineties with the possibility of thunderstorms or worse. By nine a.m. the men were sweating and looking for cold drinks.

The ladies didn't much care about weather predictions or the heat. They had gotten up early and were at the upscale shopping and dining mall, *The Somerset Collection,* when the doors opened at ten a.m. They would be shopping, walking, talking, and eating, all in expansive, two and three storied, marbled floor, air-conditioned comfort.

Katherine felt bad for Alexander's sister, Lisa Burgess, when after a three cocktail lunch, her sisters thought shopping for lingerie would be high entertainment. Lisa, who had only one drink, led them to *Soma Intimates* and had Katherine try on a lace gown and then a demure chemise. Her sisters told Lisa those were very nice and in such good taste, but then grabbed Katherine by both arms and led her down the mall to Victoria's Secret.

Soon they were all laughing and catcalling as they made her try on the most revealing lingerie they could find. Sheer baby doll. Lisa whispered, "Oh my!" Peek-a-boo bikini. "Oh my!" Open halter. G-string and tassels. See-thru body stocking. "Oh my! Oh my! Oh my!" Lisa repeated. Then, "Let me look at that." Katherine's sisters had a way of loosening you up. They all chipped in and bought her seven sexy pieces.

"One for each night of your honeymoon," they said.

"Be sure to order a wheel chair for Alex on your return flight. You're goin' to wear that boy out," Kristen said.

Lisa frowned, put her hands over her ears and changed, "La la la la. I don't want to hear this."

~~~

The men got their last round of golf in at the country club just as the wind started to pick up. On the last six holes, all of their drives were getting hooked into the trees with gusts up to thirty miles an hour. They were glad to get inside and cool off. The barbecue on the deck was taken inside due to the developing thunderstorms and the boys changed into their dressy casual attire. Mr. Burgess joined them around 6:00 p.m. after a long day in the financial markets, reporting some dark and foreboding clouds coming in from the west. His son thought he meant financial rather than weather until his father said there were some funnel clouds reported south of Lansing and headed their way. Katherine's father was unable to attend due to securing equipment and animals for the incoming storm. Just as Mr. Burgess was about to make a toast to his son, a bolt of lightning struck nearby and the power went out.

~~~

The bride and groom of the Friday evening wedding and their attendants scampered into their limo after an hour of family pictures in the chancel of the First Presbyterian Church. Pastor Stewart advised them that the weather warning radio had gone off in the sacristy with a tornado warning from the national weather service. Funnel clouds had been spotted over Milford and were headed for Bloomfield Hills. Pouring rain and constant lightning strikes ensued as they pulled out of the drive and headed up Woodward to the Iroquois Club two miles north of the church. By the time they arrived, the power was out and a torrential rain was pelting the limo.

Stephen M. Goodrum

The Disaster

Stephen M. Goodrum

Chapter Three

Pastor Stewart closed and locked the back door and ran to his Cadillac as the wind swirled around him and the rain came in sheets. Before he started his car, he heard the emergency sirens go off. He didn't know whether he should stay in his car or head to the basement of the church. Just as he was about to get out and run for safety, rain engulfed the car and the wind suddenly started screaming like a jet engine. He felt the car spinning and lifting off the ground.

He couldn't catch his breath and a dull ache began to grow in his chest. The ache turned into a sharp pain, then numbness in his left arm as he bent over and grabbed the steering wheel. It felt like the wind had sucked all of the oxygen out of the car. He knew he was having a heart attack. He said a quick prayer and whispered to his wife that he loved her.

The car seemed to be spinning higher off the ground and flipping to its side when something exploded through the windshield, hit the passenger seat and drove the car down and backward, crashing it to the ground. The air bag went off pinning him to the seat. When it deflated, he raised his hands up over his eyes as the rain turned into needles pelting his face. He heard chunks of debris hitting the roof and sides of the car, then a loud wrenching scraping sound that ended in a crash somewhere in front of him.

The wind stopped, the rain subsided and the sun shone through the clouds. He felt some relief in his chest as he gulped in air that carried the scent of ozone. He slowly opened his eyes, wiping what felt like sand from his face that left blood dripping down his hands. He looked out the windshield and gasped. The top of the five story stone bell tower had fallen into the driveway and landed only a few feet from the front of the car.

He turned to his right and with unbelieving eyes saw what had crashed through the windshield, tore away the passenger seat and drove the car back and down to the ground: the six foot tall marble sanctuary statue of Jesus minus the shepherd's staff and sheep. "Jesus H. Christ!" he screamed, and passed out. From that day forward, he was known to proclaim "Jesus saves!" like a good southern Baptist.

He came-to a few minutes later and realized his leg was broken and he couldn't get out of the car. He tried to find his cell phone, but all he could see in the seat was pellets of glass. He looked up and saw that somehow the OnStar system was still intact and pushed the call button. A calm woman's voice came over the speaker: "This is OnStar, I see you have experience a front end collision and the air bag was deployed. The police have been dispatched and are on their way. How else may I help you this evening, Pastor Stewart?"

"I've been hit by a tornado and I'm having a heart attack. I'm trapped in my car in the back parking lot of the church, but I think the main driveway is blocked."

"Okay, Pastor Stewart. Hold on. Remain calm. I've called EMS and they are on their way."

OnStar stayed on the line until they heard the sirens of the Bloomfield Township Emergency Rescue truck. He asked the woman to dial his wife and tell her what had happened. He heard his wife invoke the name of God and said she was glad he was still alive. He interrupted the conversation and said," Yes, my Dear, Jesus literally saved me. He's sitting next to me here in the car." His wife thought he must be having some kind of religious experience, told him everything would be alright and she would meet him at the hospital.

EMS took his vitals in the car, put an oxygen mask on his face and started an IV while. Once they rescued him from the car, they put him on a collapsible stretcher and loaded him into the ambulance. As they drove out of the lot, he asked them how much damage had the church endured. They told him not to worry, not wanting to cause him any more stress. They didn't think it was a good idea to tell him that half the church's roof was hanging down the side of the building with the entire stone bell tower lying in the driveway. There would be no Saturday weddings or Sunday services for the remainder of the year.

A quarter of mile wide swath of destruction had swept through Oakland County starting at Commerce Township just east of Milford, missing the Huron Valley Hospital, but destroying million dollar homes along the south side of Orchard Lake and up Long Lake Road where the Presbyterian Church was now in shambles. It missed the roof of the Bloomfield Hills Country Club, but tore up several fairways and blew out the windows in the Clubhouse and Sunroom, pouring horizontal rain through the building and shorting out all of the appliances. There would be no dinners or wedding receptions for at least the next week.

At seven o'clock, Mrs. Beatrice Burgess received a call from Reverend Eunice Middleton about the disaster at the church and Pastor Stewart's condition. She answered "Thank you," and passed out. The evening maid found her on the floor in the den, got her on the couch and used smelling salts to revive her. The maid called Mr. Burgess who was still at the Country Club with Alexander and the groomsmen. Beatrice was coherent enough to tell her husband what happened at the church, that the wedding would be a disaster, and passed out again.

Eugene hung up the phone, ironically glad that his wife passed out and he didn't have to tell her about the damage at the Country Club. One shock at a time.

He stood quietly for several minutes in the dimness of the safety lights. He wasn't sure what he should do first: call in some favors from other members of the country club to find a church, or tell his son what had happened. Thinking that all of the neighboring churches would be having weddings this weekend, he decided to talk to Alexander.

After the explosion of the windows and the driving rain subsided, Alex and the boys decided to play cards in the poker room by lantern light. Mr. Burgess walked in and called Alexander over for a private conversation. When Alex saw the look on his father's face, he asked, "What is it, Father? Is everything alright?"

"Alexander, something has happened."

"Is anybody hurt?"

"No. Everyone is fine."

"Okay. Good. What's wrong?"

"The tornado that came through here tore off the roof and the bell tower of the church. Pastor Stewart had a mild heart attack and is now resting at Beaumont Hospital."

"Oh my God," said Alex. "Does Katherine know yet?"

"No. They haven't arrived at the house yet. Your mother passed out, but Marion is getting her up to bed to rest."

"Holy shit!" said Alex.

"No shit," replied his father.

"We've got to figure what we can do before Katie finds out," Alex said.

"Right, right," Eugene answered. "I think I'm in shock. I can't think of a thing."

Alex and his father walked back to the poker table and stopped the game. "Boys," exclaimed Alex, "we have a problem. The church lost its roof and the pastor is in the hospital. There's going to be no wedding at First Presbyterian. We need to come up with a new plan, and now!"

"You got it," the men replied in unison.

"We'll figure something out, Dad," Alex told his father

"I sure hope so," Mr. Burgess replied, "or we'll be having a funeral for my wife next week."

~~~

The girls were just finishing their low-cal desserts at *J. Alexander's* when Katherine received the call from Alex. She sat perfectly still, gasping at every new detail of the night's events. She suddenly burst into tears. "Oh, God! Oh, God! Zander, *Zander*, my wedding day is ruined." The bridesmaids heard and quickly got up from their chairs and circled the wagons, offering tissues and hugs, and questions about what was going on.

"Listen Katie. Katie? Listen, Honey. We'll work something out, okay?"

"Zander, Zander," she cried. "My perfect wedding day, it's, it's a disaster!" She blew her nose and grabbed more tissue. "Can, can we postpone?"

"No, honey. The church won't be ready till who know when, and we already have the license, and I don't want to live at home another day, or stay over at your parent's house."

Katherine blew her nose again. "Okay, okay Dear. You talk with the guys and I'll let the girls know and see what we can come up with."

"That's the spirit, Honey. Now, stay with the girls, talk things out and I'll call you back later. We're still going to have a wedding. And most importantly, we're still going to get married, tomorrow. And, Katie?"

"Yes, dear?" she said between sobs.

"I love you."

"I love you too," she said, hung up the phone and blew her nose.

Her oldest sister, Kristen, sitting next to her, took her hand and asked, "What's wrong, Katie? What happened? Did that man get cold feet and run?"

Katherine composed herself, blew her nose one more time and looked at her sister. "No, dummy. It's not Zander. It's the church. It's the country club. You know that thunder we were hearing. Well, they got hit by a tornado and the pastor had a heart attack. There's no church, no minister, no reception, and..." she squeezed her eyes shut and started to cry, "no wedding." She burst into tears.

The rest of the bridesmaids gasped in shock and starting crying with her.

Kristen noticed the people sitting around them were staring and whispering. The staff had come up to see what was going on. She told Alex's sister, Lisa, to call up the limo. She directed her other two sisters, Kylee and Korinne, to take Katie to the restroom and wash her face and freshen up her makeup.

As the table cleared, Kristen paid the bill and called her mother. She explained what had happened and asked her the most important question of the evening. She heard her mother cover the phone and call out to their

41

daddy. She could hear them confer and then heard her dad say, "Of course." Her mother told her the answer she knew they would give. She hung up with a smile. The Hatfields would never let Michigan weather come between their little sister and happiness.

Her sisters brought Katie out of the restroom, through the restaurant and to the door as the limo pulled up in front. Kristen whispered to Kylee and Korinne as they climbed in the stretched SUV. Once everyone was seated, the sisters nodded to one another in agreement.

"I called Mom and Pop," Kristen announced. "And they said they will take care of everything. You're still going to have your weddin', little sister."

"Really?" Katie asked with hope. "Oh, thank God." She fell back into her seat. "Wait! What are they going to do?"

"We're going to have a country wedding at our house!" she answered proudly.

"Oh, God!" Katie replied.

"Now you know our parents are not going to embarrass you in front of the Burgesses."

"I don't know, Kristen. You don't know these people. And speaking of people, how will we let everyone know?"

"Mom's gettin' on the ol' church phone tree. Apparently Reverend Eunice's goin' to do the same for the Presbyterians."

"Okay.

"Now, don't you worry about a thing Katee-Mae. And to help you to be care free, we're now going to show you a gooood time."

At this, Kristen moved up front and told the driver where to go. Kylee and Korinne poured drinks and gave Katie an extra strong one.

Lisa Burgess sat stone still taking all of this in, wondering if her mother had survived the news. Kylee passed her a drink and asked if she was alright. She smiled back at her and said, "I think I'm better now than I was half a hour ago, and I think everything's going to turn out alright.

"You think?" Katie asked. "What about your mother? She's not going to like this one bit."

"Don't worry about my mom. No Presbyterian Church and no County Club? The worst is over. She'll just be glad to get this weekend over with and put it behind her. I really think, Katherine, I mean, Kadee-Mae, you and my brother, I mean, Zander, are finally going to *enjoy* your wedding day.

"Not to mention *the night*," Kylee said.

Chapter Four

The limo driver pulled out onto Big Beaver and headed east toward Mt. Clemens. He knew right where to go. He'd taken other bachelorette parties to Jake's, but he never expected this sedate group of well coiffed women to end up there. Then he heard the girls put on Donna Summer singing *"Hot Stuff,"* and knew that their prim and proper looks were deceiving. Yes, they were *wantin' some hot stuff this evening.*

~~~

Alex gathered the groomsmen around him, found a legal pad in a cupboard and got out his pen, ready to write down any and all good ideas. His best man said, "How about another golf club. I know one that does weddings." He called and found out that they were booked solid.

Just then, one of Katie's brothers, Kyle, got a call from the oldest sister. As he listened, he held up his hand. "Okay, okay. Great! I'll let Alex know. Yep. Okay. Where

45

are you guys? Headed where? Sorry. None of my business. Okay, bye."

"That was my sister Kristen. The wedding is taken care of. Our mom and pop have offered the farm for the wedding, and they'll even find a minister." The room erupted in cheers. Alex high-fived Kyle, Katie's other brother, and Kal, her younger brother, thanking them for their family's offer. He could relax now. He sat back down and let out a big sigh of relief. He then watched his father pull out his phone and call home to tell his mother the *good news.* From the look on his father's face, he didn't think she saw it that way.

The boys ordered another round of drinks and started a new hand of poker. Alex's father motioned him out of the room. "I spoke to your mother. When I told her that the wedding was going to be at Katherine's parent's farm, she passed out, again."

"She's just still in shock about the church, Dad."

"Maybe," his dad answered. "I called Reverend Middleton to see if she could perform the ceremony, but she said she was already presiding over a wedding at some banquet hall in Pontiac. She also said that the choir was also unavailable. Apparently Director Wolfgang won't have his semi-professional singers perform without the pipe organ. It was their trademark or something. So, at this point, we have a wedding on a farm with a country preacher and no music. It just doesn't sound very elegant, Alex. And your mother has expected elegant all of her life."

"It's just not '*decently and in order*,' right Father?" Alex asked.

"That's not it at all, Son."

"Well, Father, if it's good enough for Katie, it's good enough for me. It's our wedding, not mother's, not yours, not the church's. Now, I'm going back in there and I'm going to tell the guys about needing music and a choir and we'll see what we can come up with. Tomorrow's going to be a beautiful day and I'm going to marry the most beautiful girl in the world. And, Dad, I think *this* wedding is finally going to be fun."

~~~

The boys finished their tenth hand of poker when Alex's brother and best man, Benjamin, pulled him aside. "I think I found our choir for the wedding. A good friend of

47

mine, Danny, is a great singer. He's sung solos at our church. I asked him if he could perform at a late afternoon wedding tomorrow out at Katherine's house. He said that not only could he be there, but he could bring his choir. They usually sing at contests at the *Pronto!* Tomorrow night, they'll be singing at *Club Esquire* in Lansing. So, he said they'll just get dressed up early, sing for the wedding and the reception then head to Lansing afterwards. How's that sound?"

"Great, I guess. So they'll be able to do it pronto?"

"Yes. And no. The name of the club is *Pronto!*"

"What's *Pronto?*" Alex asked.

"It's just a dinner and dance club in Royal Oak," Benjamin answered. "Apparently they have talent contests. Look, this Danny is a professional singer. He has the voice of an angel. Our family will be very impressed with him, and I'm sure his men's group, they're called the *Ange Fee Choir*, are as good as he is, or he wouldn't be singing with them. We would just need to find a DJ with a sound system so everyone could hear."

"Sounds good," Alex said. He told everyone at the table the good news. Katie's older brother, Kyle, asked where they were from.

"*Pronto!* in Royal Oak," Benjamin answered. Kyle smothered a laugh and said, "Great!" He turned to his brother and whispered something. They turned their heads away and laughed.

"What's up guys?" Alex asked.

"Nothing, Alex," Kyle said. "Don't worry about a sound system, we got one. Just have Danny and his choir bring an iPod with their music on it. Now, how about we split this pop-stand and me and my bro take you out for a drink. You can stay overnight at the farm, and in the morning give you the lay of the land for the ceremony tomorrow. What ya think."

"Sounds good. Benjamin? Why don't you call your sister and tell her the details on the choir and let Katie know we've got the music covered."

"Will do, Alex."

Alex told his father he was going out with the Hatfield brothers and he'd stay out at their house tonight. His father pointed at Benjamin and motioned him over.

"You go along and watch out for Alex. Your mother and I will see you in the morning. And, Benjamin? Alex? No shenanigans tonight."

"Yes, Father," they answered in unison, giving him a lame salute.

Alex told the Hatfields that Benjamin was coming along for the night.

The Hatfields smiled and said, "Cool!"

~~~

The girls pulled up to Jake's on Gratiot Avenue and piled out of the car and into the nightclub. Kristen spoke with a woman at a lectern with a seating chart, handed her a wad of cash, and a girl led them to a back room. Katie saw that there was something special going on tonight, but she missed what was on the marquee.

The girls maneuvered their way through a boisterous crowd around the bar to an adjacent room that must have been an old theater. The smell of beer, martinis, margaritas, perfume, sweat and hair spray filled the air. Near the stage, Katie noticed that there were group of women in front, each one with a woman wearing a short white veil and a wedding rehearsal bouquet. She saw a couple more in the second row and thought this must be some kind of bridal show. Kristen ushered their group down to the front row as the lights went down and the traditional bridal march began. A girl in a skimpy waitress outfit handed them tall flutes with Champagne and told Katie, "Congratulations." Then with a wink, she said, "Enjoy the show."

The curtain opened and there stood an entire bridal party with six beautifully dressed women in matching bridesmaid's gowns standing on the left and six handsome men in tailored black tuxes standing on the right. In the middle stood a handsome, sexy man dressed in black tails and top hat holding hands with a woman in a red glitter jacket and miniskirt suit holding a microphone.

"Welcome to the *Bridal Show*, girls. Let me see the hands of our brides."

Katie waved her hand in the air with the other brides in the audience. Everyone cheered.

The MC started walking provocatively across the stage. "Our attendants are all here, and we have our stand-in groom, but as you can see, we're missing a bride. So, which one of you lucky girls soon to be married would like to come up on stage and be our special guest?"

A group of women pushed a girl with a short veil from the front row up to the stage as everyone whooped and hollered. Katie was cheering and laughing along with everyone else, realizing this wasn't just a fashion show.

The music changed to a thumping beat and the wedding party started dancing with arms swaying in the air and hips swinging. The groom came forward, ripped off his jacket revealing sculpted arms, a tight six pack and a bulge in his low-riding pants. He grabbed the bride's hands and began dancing with her, gyrating his hips to the suggestive beat. The room erupted into catcalls and lewd remarks. Katie looked at her sisters and broke out in a sweat. They were all clapping their hands and nodding their heads and motioning for her to go up on stage.

The first bride was handed down to the groomsmen who were now without their jackets, topless like the groom. Katie's sisters grabbed her drink, pulled her out of her chair and pushed her up to the front. The groom grabbed her hands, pulled her up on stage and started the same sexy dance with her. She screamed with delight as the groom flipped her around and moved in close behind her. Her head began to spin as he put his hands around her waist and brought his head down and kissed her on the neck. She could hear her sisters yelling and screaming her name as the groom started humping her from behind.

He spun her away toward the groomsmen and she saw they no longer had any pants on.

She was grabbed by the best man, picked her up under her arms, causing her legs to wrap around his hips. He danced around in circles, letting her down to the stage on her knees. The next groomsmen moved in close and began thrusting his well endowed crotch toward her face. He pulled her up to her feet and swung her around by her arms, the spotlights spinning above her making her dizzy. She suddenly became light headed and started seeing stars. The last thing she remembered was one of the groomsman catching her against his sweaty chest, picking her up and throwing her over his shoulder. She puked up dinner down his back and passed out.

~~~

"So, where we going now?" Benjamin asked as the SUV merged off I-696 onto I-96 north-west of Detroit.

"Just out for another drink," Kyle said with a smile on his face.

"Oh, okay," Benjamin said.

"Yeah, relax Ben," said Alex. "We're with my new family. Right boys?"

"That's right. And we're goin to treat you like family," Kyle said, driving the SUV south on US-23 past Ann Arbor, exiting on Michigan Avenue. Twenty minutes later he pulled into a packed parking lot of a bar called *The Hills*. No doubt, thought Alex, named after the area, Irish Hills.

"I didn't expect such a big place out in the middle of the country," said Alex.

"It's big because it's popular with us country boys, and its ten minutes from the Michigan Speedway. You been to a NASCAR race?" Kyle asked.

"Can't say that I have," said Alex.

"Well, we'll be takin' you there next year. We're goin' on Sunday. We're big Junior fans," Kyle said.

"*Junior*?" Ben asked

"Dale Earnhardt, Jr., race car driver."

"Oh, yeah. Seen him in a commercial on TV," Ben answered.

"Right," said Kyle. "In August, we'll introduce you to him in person. We're part of his fan club and we got VIP passes."

"Oh, good," Ben replied.

Everyone climbed out of the car and walked into the night club. They were hit by the noise of hundreds of voices and the pulse of loud music, *My Last Name,* sung by Carrie Underwood. Kyle and Kal led Alex and Ben to a room adjacent to the bar where groups of men were gathering. At the front was a small stage with a band set up to play.

"Good deal. We made it for the late show," Kal said.

After ordering beers, Kyle said, "You boys are gonna enjoy this country band."

"Great," said Alex. "But I really need to get to bed soon, Kyle. How long we gonna be here?" Alex realized he was starting to talk like the Hatfields.

"Just for the show. About an hour. Trust me, you'll be glad you did," Kyle answered.

Over the growing noise of men's conversations, a voice boomed over the stage speakers. "Gentlemen, and Ladies, Welcome to *The Hills.*" A cheer went up from the crowd.

I'd like to introduce to you the band, who for you regulars, need no introduction: *The,* all *wo-man, Cowgirl Band.*" The room erupted in hoots and whistles.

Five women sauntered out in halter tops, leather chaps and silver-studded pink cowgirl boots. A blond, Jessica Simpson look-a-like wearing a leather vest and pants suit stood in front of the microphone and nodded to the drummer. A steady, stomping beat started as the base guitar played a deliberate descending run that everyone recognized as intro to *These Boots Are Made For Walking*.

The singer started swaying to the beat and looking into the audience. Kyle pointed out Alex, pulled him out of his chair and pushed him up the steps to the stage. The singer extended her hand to him and belted out:

"You keep saying you got somethin' for me (uh)."

She grabbed his arm and pulled him closer.

"Something you call love, but confess.

You've been messin' where you shouldn't

been a messin'

and now someone else is gettin'

all your best."

She ripped off her pants to reveal a pair of leather *Daisy Dukes*.

"These boots are made for walkin'.

And that's just what they'll do

One of these days these boots are gonna

walk all over you."

The entire room was standing and hollering and she turned around and took off her vest revealing she had nothing on. She turned back twirling two tassels with each stomp of her boots. She pushed Alex into a folding chair that appeared out of nowhere.. She started the lyrics again, this time toward Alex.

"You keep saying you got something

for me (uh)"

She tugged on his belt.

"Well sir, I don't mind to say you do."

She undid his belt, lifted his chin and pulled his head to her tassels/

"Now you're looking right where I

thought you'd be looking."

She swung her hips around and pushed her bare butt cheeks toward Alex's face.

"Legs come handy when a man's

in front of you."

She started stomping one boot after another, each cheek bouncing to the beat.

"These boots are made for walkin'

and that's just what they'll do.
One of these days these boots are gonna
walk all over you."

She quickly bent over and backed into Alex's crotch just as his pants fell to his shoes. The room erupted in cheers and whistles as she pushed her bottom up and down on his underwear.

Alex tried to back away, but the chair wouldn't move and he fell backward onto the floor. The stripper turned around and straddled him and swung her hand around in the air like riding a bronco: Alex's eyes were going round and round as he saw her tassels swing in front of him. Soon, he was so dizzy, he dropped his head to the floor, knocking himself out cold. He didn't hear the room yell their approval or the see the Hatfields run up on stage, pick him up and carry him out of the room to wild cheers.

The Wedding Day

Stephen M. Goodrum

Chapter Five

Alex woke up the next morning with a bright light shining in his face. He raised his head shading his eyes to look around and see where he could be, hoping it wasn't the spotlight on the stage. His eyes adjusted to the room and he realized it was sunlight streaming in the window in an upstairs bedroom of the Hatfields' farmhouse.

He felt a dull pain in the back of his head. He reached around to rub it, but when he touched it, a sharp pain shot from the back to the front of his head. He slowly laid his head back on the pillow and closed his eyes. He saw tassels swirling around and remembered what had happened at the bar. He opened his eyes again, this time away from the window. He hoped he could get the sight of swirling tassels out of his mind before the wedding. It wouldn't be right to get married with that on his mind.

He reached around to the back of his head again and found a knot that hurt to the slightest touch. He must have hit the stage floor when he flipped his head away from the... there they were again... the tassels. *Dear God*.

He slid his feet off the bed keeping his head as low as possible, thinking if he could get on all fours, he could crawl to the bathroom without too much pain. Off the bed, he looked down and saw that he still had his dress pants on but no shirt. He crawled to the bathroom and made it to the john in time to pee bent over the commode holding onto the tank.

He flushed and ever so slowly pushed himself upright, keeping his eyes closed until the pounding behind his skull subsided. He turned around to walk out and caught a glimpse of himself in a full length mirror on the bathroom door. He saw a red stripe starting as his navel, then sliding into his pants. He unzipped, pulled down his trousers and underwear and saw the stripe's bottom half. It was an arrow pointing downward stopping just above his hair line. Looking back up, he saw block letters printed above his belly button that read backwards: DOWN HERE!

"Great."

He closed his eyes and rubbed his hands over his face and his knuckles in his eyes and looked again. Yep, they were still there. He looked away.

Next to the bathroom door he saw a pink shower curtain around a tub. He stripped off his pants and underwear, turned on the water, pulled the shower control, stepped in and got on all fours.

The water started ice cold and he tried to jump back. A pain shot through his head with the quick movement, so he closed his eyes and stopped. He reached around like a blind man until he found the hot water knob and turned it on until it was steamy hot. He sat down in the tub and let the shower wash over his neck and shoulders. He found some body wash and soaped up. When he got to his belly, he scrubbed as hard as he could, but the soap didn't even touch the block letters or the arrow. He needed a stronger detergent. That's when he noticed that the suds had a sweet strawberry scent. The shower curtain had flowers on the pink background and the tub was lined with a variety of feminine soaps, shampoos, body wash, shaving cream and a pink razor.

"Oh Shit" Whose bathroom was he in? Whose shower was he using?

He turned off the shower and heard someone outside the door.

"Korinne? Is that you honey?" Karen Hatfield called out.

Oh my God, Alex thought.

He got up with a shooting pain, but found a fluffy pink towel and quickly wrapped it around his waist. He cleared his throat and said, "It's me, Mrs. Hatfield, Alex."

"Oh? Oh! What are you doing in Korinne's bathroom, Alex?"

"I don't know. I mean, I woke up in her bedroom and I had to use the bathroom and I didn't know it was her room."

"Well, whose room did you *think* it was, Alex? Katie Mae's?"

"No! No, Ma'am. I didn't know whose room it was." He waited for a response, but only heard what sounded like a snicker on the other side of the door.

"You didn't sleep with Katie's little sister did you?"

"Oh, no! No Ma'am. I don't want you to think that I would ever do anything like that, Ma'am. I just woke up by myself. I really didn't know where I was," Alex answered. He waited again and heard another snicker, then someone else snickering.

"Well, I should hope not, young man. I'm going to find Korinne right now and have a little talk with her. Now, I'm not going to mention this to Katie Mae. I'd hate for her to find out anything like this on her wedding day."

Alex heard muffled laughter.

"Nothing happened, Ma'am. Nothing at all."

"Okay, if you say so, Alex. I'll be going now."

He heard steps walk away from the door then out and out laughter down the hallway.

He slowly stood up, grabbed a towel, pink, and dried off. He stepped out of the tub in time to hear a knock on the door.

"Who is it?"

"It's Kyle."

"Come in."

He opened the door, walked in, saw Alex with the towel around him and said, "Why, look at you, Mr. Pretty in pink."

"Right. Look, Kyle, how'd I get here?" Alex asked.

"We brought you to our house. Don't you remember?"

The tassels swirled back into his vision. "All too well, Kyle. All too well. But, I mean, how'd I get in Korinne's bedroom."

"Me and Kal carried you upstairs. You were dead weight, so we dropped you in the nearest bed with nobody in it. Besides, all the girls are bunking together in

Katie's room around the corner, and I was given strict instructions to not let you see Katie all day until the wedding."

"Oh, okay. Great. Hey, I need some clothes," Alex said.

"Put on what you had on yesterday."

"I need some clean underwear, and a shirt. And check this out," Alex said as he opened the towel, showing his stomach.

"Wow, look at that. You got something written on your belly."

"No shit, Sherlock. Did you guys put that there?" Alex asked.

"Who, us?. What's that say? *Down Here?*'" Kyle started laughing.

Kal walked in and saw that Alex had found their handiwork and started laughing with Kyle.

"You guys," Alex said.

"Don't worry, Dude. It'll come off. Eventually." More laughter.

"What did you use?"

"Just some magic marker," Kyle answered.

"Was it permanent?" Alex asked.

"Don't know," Kal answered. "Didn't look."

"Great. Thanks guys."

"You're welcome. It's more of joke on Katie than you," Kyle said.

"I'm sure she'll be laughing," Alex said.

"Come on Kal," Kyle said. "Let's leave Alex here to his, uh, *private* moment. And get him some clothes. Don't want anyone to see him like this."

"Okay. Be right back, Alex."

"Could you please not tell anyone about this?" Alex asked. He wasn't about to tell them that their mom questioned him about being in Korinne's room and shower, and then accusing him of sleeping with her. He would never hear the end of it.

"Yeah, sure Alex," Kyle said. "Mum's the word."

~~~

Katie woke up to the sound of her sisters giggling. She raised herself on her elbows and saw Kristen and Korinne standing together beside her bed.

"It's your wedding day, Katie Mae," said Kristen.

"Up and at 'em, or should I say, up and Alex," Korinne said with another giggle.

Katie threw back the covers, shifted her feet to the floor and felt the room spin around for a minute. "What did you guys give me to drink last night?"

"You don't remember?" asked Korinne.

The sight of a black pouch barely concealing *Johnson and the twins* danced across her mind's eye. "Oh yes, I remember last night, that is, until I passed out. And I've never passed out from drinking. So what was in that drink? What did you give me?"

"Just a Harvey Walbanger," said Kristen. "We thought it was an appropriate drink for the *Bridal Show*. Must have had a double of Mr. Vodka."

"Thanks a lot. And you call that a bridal show? I expected models in bridal wear, or maybe a funny skit." Katie said.

"Oh, there were models in bridal wear. Good lookin' boys in tuxes. And there was a funny skit. It's just you didn't see much of it because you were in it," Kristen said."

"Very funny," Katie said.

"Did you enjoy, ahem, *the show*, Katie Mae?" asked Korinne

"I need a shower," answered Katie, trying to dismiss the sight of the *groom's* thrusting crotch.

"And then it's off to the beauty salon," Korinne said. "And maybe a little shopping too."

~~~

Outside, Mr. Horatio Hatfield was mowing the field on the other side of the driveway for parking. He directed the boys to weed whack around the house and the barn as a couple of neighbor men were constructing an arbor in front of the house under two large shade trees. Mrs. Karen Hatfield was in her garden picking the flowers that would lace the arbor for the wedding as well as Katie's dress. Horatio and Karen were determined to make her wedding the most beautiful and elegant country wedding possible.

Earlier in the morning Karen had called up their church's women's league to cook everything from fried chicken to homemade cherry pie for the outdoor reception. The Women's League of the Irish Hills Free Will

Baptist Church of Norvell Township was well known for their cooking prowess, more than one of the members always winning first place at the Jackson County Fair. Cooking for several hundred people would not be a problem for these women, as easy as one of their prize-winning pies.

Alex was in the Hatfields' modern equipped kitchen, eating a bacon cheese omelet with fresh squeezed orange juice and black coffee. He was also consuming as much water as he could to try to ease his hangover. Korinne came down the back stairs, saw him and screamed. She made a u-turn and yelled at Kristen to stop Katie from coming down the stairs.

"You get out on the back porch, Buster. You're not allowed to see the bride on her wedding day until she walks down the aisle. Now get movin."

"Korinne! Korinne?" Alex thought he'd better warn her about Mrs. Hatfield discovering him in her bathroom and using her bed for the night. Korinne ran back down into the kitchen.

"What? Need a kick in the butt? Get out of this room. Right now," she said pointing her finger toward the door.

"Okay, okay. I'm going," Alex said. He grabbed Korinne's arm and pulled her along with him. "Listen. I've got to tell you something."

"What? And keep moving." She took his hand and pulled him into the wide back porch overlooking a large brick patio, expansive backyard, a barn and a cornfield beyond.

"I woke up in your bedroom and while I was using your shower, your mom walked in and found me in your bathroom."

Korinne smothered a smile and said, "She saw you neked?"

"No, no. Nothing like that, I don't think. She thought it was you. When she found out it was me, she thought I had *slept* with you. So you've got to tell her that that isn't true."

"Slept with me?" she said. "Alex, you shouldn't be thinkin' dirty thoughts like that on your weddin' day."

"Ssh. Ssh, quiet," Alex said in a loud whisper. "I wasn't thinking about you."

"Well!" Korinne said, putting her hands on her hips. "You don't think you could get off thinkin' 'bout me?"

"No. I mean, yes. I could, but I don't, won't, not that I couldn't. Oh Korinne."

How do women get me mixed up like this.

"Your mother accused me of sleeping with you. So, you've got to tell her it isn't true. Okay?"

Korinne could no longer keep a straight face, so she gave Alex a big smile, raised and wagged her index finger back and forth and said, "I'll never tell." She gave Alex a kiss on the cheek and ran up the stairs giggling.

"Great," said Alex, shaking his head. He rubbed his face with both hands and brushed back his hair, only to accidentally rub the knot on the back of his head. "Ow!"

Korinne called back down the stairs, "We're going out the front, Alex *love*. Stay in the back of the house."

"Yes, Ma'am."

Alex heard the clatter of women's shoes running down the front stairwell and out the front door. He heard Kristen's Mustang convertible roar to life and peel out down the driveway.

The girls were whooping it up as they flew down the drive, waving at their dad. When they got to the gravel road, Kristen took a sharp turn, slid the back tires sideways and almost lost control. The road was slick and muddy from the torrential rains the night before. She punched the accelerator and straightened out the car from the skid. "Put your seat belts on girls," she yelled. "We're goin' to town."

Katie was in the back seat with Korinne, holding her head as she swayed back and forth from Kristen's driving. "Please slow down. My head still hurts."

"Sorry, honey," said Kristen. "We've got an appointment at the spa. When they get done with you, you will be sooo relaxed, feel sooo good, and be sooo bee-yu-tiful."

"Great," said Katie. "Just get me there in one piece."

Chapter Six

Alex finished his breakfast omelet and coffee on the back porch, and wondered where they put his brother, Ben. He started for the kitchen just as Katie's mom came in the side door to the porch with two large white plastic buckets of flowers. "Hi there, Alex. Stayin' out of trouble?"

Alex couldn't tell if she was serious or not since she had a little chicken grin on her face. "I'm being a good boy, Mrs. Hatfield."

"Good boy," she said like she was talking to a dog. "Now, startin' today, you can call me Mom. We're gonna be family in about seven hours, so... Oh my God. Seven hours."

"What can I do to help, Mrs. Ha.., uh, Mom?"

"Well let me see. First go upstairs and get your brother up and feed him some breakfast. Then, why don't you two go out and find Mr. Ha.., I mean, Horatio, and see what needs to be done. I'm sure he'll find something that needs to be done right away."

"Okay, Ma'am, I mean, Mom. I'll do that."

"And, by the way, Alex."

Oh boy, here it comes. "Yes?"

"We call Mr. Hatfield *Pop*. You can call him that too. Okay?"

Phew. "Yes, Mom. Thank You."

"Oh, loosen up, Alex. I know you didn't sleep with Korinne. She was sleepin' with her sisters after they got home about two in the morning. I think that's when she went to her room to get her nightgown and found you in her room. She said she saw that you had some kind of gift for Katie on your weddin' night."

"Oh! I mean, oh, yes. It's very nice." *Great. Now all the girls know.*

"Well, you don't have to tell me what it is. If it's somethin' for your weddin' night, I'm sure it's very special."

"Yes. She's right. It's very special. I'm sure Katie will love it." *Like hell she will. She'll probably scrub my skin raw trying to get it off.*

Karen Hatfield couldn't hide the grin on her face as she turned to go in the kitchen. "And Alex. Pop's other nick name is *Ratio*. It's short for his name, and, besides, he's quite good with math."

"Okay, Mom. Pop, or Ratio. Will do. I'll go get my brother now and we'll find Pop and see what we can do to help out."

~~~

Alex placed his empty plate and coffee cup in the kitchen sink and headed back upstairs to find his brother.

The Hatfield house was really a Victorian mansion with ornate carved wood and real plaster walls and ceilings that you tell was original work. He had only been here twice before, Thanksgiving and Christmas, and that was only in the expansive parlor for Christmas carols and gift giving, and the dining room with its solid oak table for the elaborate turkey and ham dinners with eight courses served by the Hatfield women.

Upstairs he started through the labyrinth of halls and rooms in the front end of the house. He first turned left and found Korinne's room just off the landing. That's probably why they put him there late last night. They only had to carry him up one long flight of stairs. Her room faced east sitting over the wide front porch, so he must be in the north end of the house. He turned back to the right and saw a long hallway leading to a room with an open door. He peaked in and found Mrs. Hat.., Mom, on a cordless phone in a library that had a lower and upper level with one of those moving ladders. There were enough books on the shelves to make the local library proud.

"That's good, Gertrude," said Karen as she nodded her head. "Yes, fifty whole chickens cut in two and then deep fried. We're doing fifty here. Yes, I know that's no problem for the League. Now, I want four bushels of potatoes peeled and roasted. The boys will grill the steaks out back and I'll find someone to go out in the field and pick the best sweet corn." She looked up and saw Alex at the door and waved him in. "I think I just found someone to take care of that."

Alex had a feeling he knew who that help was going to be, and he didn't know sweet corn from popcorn. He gave Mrs. Hatfield a little wave and whispered that he was looking for his brother Ben.

Karen pointed upstairs and continued her conversation. "Mabel is handling all of the desserts. She'll be at the church shortly and she'll need all of the ovens. That's why I wanted you to deep fry the chickens, not bake them. Besides, we all know, don't we Gertrude, that chicken is best fried."

Alex walked out of the room and headed back to the landing. The rest of the south side of the house must be Katie's mom and dad's master suite. She had told him when they went on their engagement trip to Florida, after they made love in their suite's hot tub, that her parents had the biggest bathroom with a large white hot tub for two. At the time, he told her he didn't want to hear about her parent's private life. She gave him a look and said, "And how do you think you got here, Buddy Boy?" He *really* didn't want to think about *that,* and her naked wet body in the bubbles drove those thoughts away pretty quickly.

Then those tassels came back into view. He shook his head and reached the stairwell. He took the next flight of stairs looking for the boy's rooms. Once again, he was confronted with a long hallway leading north, but only a short hallway leading south. This must be where the library and the master suite took up two stories. He took a left, walked to the first door and knocked. He heard rustling, footsteps and then his brother's voice asking who it was.

"It's me, Ben," Alex said.

"Who's me?" Ben asked.

"Your brother Alex. Open the door."

Ben cracked the door and looked into the hallway. When he saw Alex, he opened it wider and let him in a large guest room. Ben went back across the room to a four poster bed and jumped up on the mattress. The room was as large as the living room of his parent's house in Bloomfield Hills. It had some of the most elaborate Victorian furniture he'd ever seen. Large, hand carved cherry wood dresser, desk, wardrobe and, of course, a king size canopied bed whose mattress and covers stood four feet off the floor. "Wow, Ben. You slept in luxury."

"Whatever, Dude. I'm still sleeping." Ben turned his head away and into the plush pillows.

"Well, you need to get up. The whole family is working hard to get ready for Katie's big wedding and we need to do our part." He heard Ben say something into the covers.

Ben turned his head back toward Alex. "You need to do our part. I did my part."

"What was that?" asked Alex.

"I called Dad late last night and told him we were staying out here for the night. They're bringing our tuxes and shit."

"I don't remember you calling?"

"In the car while you were passed out with an ice bag on your head."

"Oh, yeah. Okay. Did you say anything to dad about last night?" Alex asked.

Ben sighed. "Like I said, I did my part and didn't say anything about *The Hills*." A smile crept across his face. "That was some place, wasn't it Alex?"

"Yeah, sure. Great time." *Here come the tassels again*.

Ben raised himself up on one elbow. "Did she actually hump you, man?"

"No. Definitely not," answered Alex. "And don't ever tell my parents or Katie what happened."

"Like I said, I'm doing my part," said Ben

"Thanks, Bro."

"Goodnight," said Ben as he dropped his head back on the pillows and pulled the covers over his head.

"Yeah, okay. I'll do *our* part." Alex saw that Ben was already back to sleep and snoring. He left the room and wondered, how much corn did Karen really need?

~~~

The girls made it off the rocky dirt road called, of all things, Hand Highway, onto the pavement of M-50 with a minimum of mud thrown up in the convertible. The torrential rains that came with the high winds yesterday left the road slick and at some points, treacherous. Kristen was glad they had the Mustang and not their mom's caddy.

They drove into downtown Brooklyn and pulled up to the Pussycat Spa. Mrs. Lucille Beal greeted the girls at the front door with her carrot orange hair, a la *I Love Lucy,* and ushered them into the bridal suite. They were greeted with the quiet sound of ethereal water music and the scent of water lilies.

Two ladies and one man were waiting to begin the process of turning ordinary looking women into beautiful models. Lucille knew these girls would not be the challenge that many women proved to be, all three were already beautiful in their own right. They introduced her to Lisa, and Lucille saw she was beautiful as well, just in a mousy sort of way. She could change that.

The first phase was what Lucille called *jungle jingle*, a fifteen minute stay in her steam room followed by a cold shower and an intense massage. Katie thought she might pass out again after five minutes of sweating out last night's drinks, but by the time they let the girls out of the milky steam, she began to feel better. As they exited the *jungle*, they were given bottles of ice cold water and then ushered into shower stalls where the water was ice cold, as in *jingle bells*. They all let out a scream as the water was turned on, but afterward commented on how refreshed they felt.

For the next phase, Lucy ushered them into a room that smelled of orange and lemon blossoms. Three massage tables stood ready. For the next thirty minutes all that could be heard was water music and the pleasurable moaning and an occasional scream of three women. When the masseuses were finished, they felt as if they wouldn't be able to walk. As they were ushered out for another shower, Kristen asked Lucy if she used recordings from the massage room for adult movies. Lucy just laughed and didn't really answer. Kristen looked back in the room for hidden cameras or microphones. She didn't want to find her or her sisters on some internet site.

Lucy called the next phase *beast and the beauty*. First, they all chose what hair style they wanted, Katie's sisters encouraging her to get the *Cinderella Princess* swept up style for her Prince Charming Alex. The women were then seated with their own stylist and mani/pedicurist, Katie getting Lucy for her appendages, and the salon's premier stylist, Bruce, for her hair and makeup. This was where Lucy and her crew turned everyday *beasts* into a glamorous *beauty*. When the work was all done, the results were spectacular. Katie, her sisters, and Lisa got up out of their salon chairs, looked in the mirrors, looked at one another, and immediately began to cry and hug one another. They quickly grabbed Kleenex to keep the tears from streaking their makeup and mascara. They looked as they had always imagined they would in a fairytale. They wept for how beautiful they looked, and they wept for the grief that life couldn't be like this every day.

Korinne liked laughter better than tears, so she interrupted the mush fest. "Hey, I got an idea. Let's get Katie a tattoo."

Everyone stopped and stared at her.

"You think that's a good idea?" Lisa asked.

"Sure," the Hatfield sisters said in unison.

"What? I don't want a tattoo," Katie said.

"Just a temporary one," Korinne said. "You know, something sweet and funny," she added.

"Oh, okay, I guess. What should it be? A butterfly? A heart?"

"Yeah, a heart," Kristen said.

"That'll be good. Where should I put it?"

"I've got an idea," Korinne answered.

Fifteen minutes later, a small red heart with ribbon arrows pointing toward it had been placed just above Katie's thong line.

When the girls were all set to leave, Lucy inquired about the wedding. Katie told her the story of the perfect wedding day disaster, and how her parents had saved the day.

Lisa added, "My brother Benjamin even found a choir that will come to the farm and sing."

"Are they from around here?" Lucy asked. "We have some good church choirs out this way."

"No. This is a professional choir. Ben said they've won singing contests in Detroit and Royal Oak. He said they're lead singer is a tenor and sings like an angel."

Bruce's ears perked up and asked, "What's the name of the choir, the singer?"

"I think he said the singer's name is Danny. The choir's called *Angel Fair,* or something like that."

"*Ange Fee*," Bruce said. "Oh, yes. They are *fab-u-lous*."

"Oh, you've heard of them?" Katie asked.

"Yes, Dear. You. Will. *Love.* Them. I know I do," he said with a sly grin.

The girls looked at each other.

"Great!" Katie said.

"Katie? Could you invite me to your wedding?" Bruce asked.

"Sure. Ceremony starts at five."

"Oh, thank you sooo much."

Katie turned to the rest of the Spa staff. "You too Lucy. And anyone else. Lots of food and drink. As you know, the Hatfields can put on a party."

"We'll all be there," Lucy said. Her staff all smiled and nodded.

Chapter Seven

Meanwhile, back at the ranch, Alex was heading out to the corn field with a stack of canvas bushel bags. His instructions were to pick three hundred ears of sweet corn. That didn't sound difficult. "Just snap off the ears from the stalk and fill the bags." Because of the heat and the extra humidity from yesterday's storm, he borrowed a t-shirt and shorts from Kal Hatfield, who didn't know Alex was going out into a corn field. If he did, Kal would have warned him that he needed to wear jeans, long sleeves and a straw hat. It only took ten minutes for Alex to understand why.

He saw a small field of short corn just behind the barn, then he saw a field of tall corn that stretched as far as the eye could see some hundred yards away. Since they were going to feed a couple of hundred hungry people, he thought tall corn would have larger ears and two hundred would be plenty. He headed to the tall corn.

He walked down a narrow path between stalks and the air changed. He smelled what he would later call *green*, and for the first time realized how close corn stalks were planted to one another. He started pulling ears of corn, having to twist them to pluck them off the stalks. It took him a while to fill his first bag.

On the second bag, he realized there was no breeze in a corn field where stalks were over six feet tall and started sweating profusely, the humidity stifling.

At four bags he began to realize why the leaves were called blades. They were sticking to his arms. When he raised them to pull and twist, then lower the ears to the bushel bag, they left paper thin cuts. Then the pollen off the tops was flying around and sticking to his hair, face, and his new wounds. Soon he was bleeding and itching everywhere.

At five bags he was sweating blood, sweat and tears. He needed help. He needed to get out of here.

As he tried to walk out of the corn, he realized he had gotten turned around and couldn't see his way back to the house. No matter which way he turned, he was surrounded by tall green stalks standing like sentinels to block his way.

He stood perfectly still to listen for Mr. Hatfields' tractor, but he couldn't hear anything but the creaking and crackling of corn drying in the late morning sun. He guessed it was true, you could hear corn grow. He tried yelling for help, but he realized after several tries that only the corn had ears that could hear him. What could he do? He remembered he had his cell phone, so he tried to call the house. No signal.

~~~

The kitchen had become a beehive of activity filled with the tantalizing aroma of chicken frying and potatoes boiling for the best mashed taters in the county. The crackling sound of grease in iron skillets was matched with the chopping staccato of garden fresh vegetables being cut up by the bushel full.

Karen had just hung up from her frequent phone call to the church where more women were baking biscuits, pies, and of course, a wedding cake, when she looked around and realized they had no corn on the cob. *Where is Alex*?

She ran outside to see if he was still picking in the sweet corn field next to the barn. He was nowhere to be seen. She had a crazy thought. Uh, oh. Surely not. She looked to the acres of field corn for the cattle and the grain mill and shivered at the thought. She ran out into the yard and grabbed Kyle who was trimming the shrubs. She told him that she thought Alex had gone to the field and now was apparently missing. Kyle whistled at Kal who was busy weed whacking. He motioned him over and they headed out to the forty acres beyond the barn.

They both stopped at the barn and put on their long coveralls and long sleeve shirts, one picking up a machete and the other a scythe. It was no time to be careful. They knew how dangerous the heat and humidity could be, especially to someone who wasn't acclimated to it like their city-slicker brother-in-law-to-be, not to mention his dehydrated state from last night. They didn't want their sister to be standing up to get married with at worst, a ghost, at the least a fainter.

The brothers found tracks leading into the field at the closest point to the barn. They followed torn-off shucks to the first bag, the second bag and then the third. The trail seemed to stop and they were undecided which way to go. Kyle decided to keep hacking west and told his younger brother, Kal, to go get their dog, Rufus. Kal was happy to oblige, wanting to get out of the stifling heat.

Kal went into the house, found a shirt of Alex's and called Rufus. The dog came running and jumping and barking. Kal led him outside to the cornfield. When he got to the edge, he let Rufus smell Alex's shirt, pointed into the cornfield and gave the command to find Alex. Rufus barked once and ran in between the rows of corn.

Alex had walked to what he thought was east, but was actually south. He had looked up at the sun for directions, but it seemed to be right on top of him. He sat down and put his head between his knees. He took his shirt and wiped the sweat from his head and face that was now dripping off him like he'd come out of the shower. Now he knew why the baseball player in *Field of Dreams* asked if the ball diamond was heaven. The corn field felt like hell. He closed his eyes and felt very sleepy.

Next thing he knew, there was a wet tongue licking his neck and head and the smell of dog breath in his face. "Rufus. You found me."

Alex stumbled to his feet and tried to follow Rufus as he ran away in what seemed the wrong direction. After a few rows, he called for Rufus to come back. The dog returned from what seemed like a different direction. He tried to follow again, but was quickly lost. He called Rufus again, but instead of the dog, he heard Kyle yell his name. Alex yelled back, but realized his voice was just a croak from the lack of moisture. When he tried again, he took a deep breath, became light headed and passed out.

Alex woke up with a start and a shiver up his spine. He was held down in waist deep cold water. He let out a scream and lifted his head to see Kyle and Kal looking down on him with concern. They had dunked him in the farm pond.

"That's cold! Stop it, guys. You trying to kill me?" Alex asked as he tried to scramble out of the murky water, only to slip and fall backward.

The brothers caught him before his head went under. "No, you're tryin' to kill your-*self*, Al. You got heat stroke, soon-to-be-brother. We can't let you get sick on your weddin' day. Lucky for you, Rufus here found you." The big black dog ran into the pond and splashed his way up to Alex, licking his face with abandon.

Alex put his hands up to his face and then pushed Rufus away. "Please take this mutt and get me out of this muddy water. I'm okay now, really. Let me go so I can take a regular shower and get dressed."

"I'll get you some shorts and a T-shirt," Kyle said.

"And I'll get you some cold water and oranges," Kal said.

"Great, great. Thanks, guys. Thanks for everything."

~~~

Karen Hatfield heard her two sons scuffle through the door. Rufus followed and shook himself, splattering water all over the floor. When she looked over to yell at her sons, she saw that they were holding someone between them.

"Who you got there?"

"It's just Alex," Kyle said.

"Yeah," Kal added. "We found him in the back cornfield. He got too hot, so we cooled him down in the pond."

"What? Alex? You alright, Dear?" Mrs. Hatfield asked as she scurried across the kitchen to take a look. What she saw, she didn't like. Alex had a red face with pasty skin.

"You come in here and sit down. I'll turn on the fan and get you somethin' to drink. You boys go on back out and help your Dad."

As they started to leave, she stopped them. "Hold on, hold on. We forgot about chairs. We need to get chairs. And we need sweet corn. So take the pickup and head over to the church. Gather up all the folding chairs you can find. Then, call me and let me know how many you got. Then go down to Lesher's Produce and get two hundred ears of corn."

"Yes, Ma'am," they said in unison. They hurried out the door, excited about driving the big Ford 250 diesel truck and raising some rocks on their country roads.

"Now, Alex, you sit right here and I'll get you some orange juice. We got to get you better before the service. Don't want Katie seein' you like this, or worse yet, you passin' out on your weddin' day."

"Yes, Ma'am."

"And quit callin' me *Ma'am*. First of all, I'm not *that* old. Second of all, you can start callin' me *Mom*, now. Hear?"

"Yes, Ma'...a, Mom."

She went to the sink and put a large wash cloth under cold water, wrung it out and put it on Alex's head. She poured some orange juice, shook some salt in it and handed it to him. "Drink that down and then we'll get you some cold water."

"Yes... Mom."

~~~

Kyle and Kal got to their small county church five miles away in about seven minutes. They slid into the parking lot and ran through the back basement door into Fellowship Hall. The smell of chicken cooking and pies baking filled the room. What it was empty of was chairs. Kyle ran into the kitchen and yelled over the chatter of a half dozen women, two of them arguing.

"Gertrude! Where's all the chairs?"

The women froze and stopped the argument over the best recipe for blueberry pie.

"Whew! You 'bout gave me a heart attack," Gertrude said. The rest of the women spoke simultaneously and nodded in agreement. From the ovens he heard, "You lookin for chairs?" Mabel walked up to the doorway.

"Yes, Ma'am, and sorry to have startled y'all," Kyle said. "The weddin's in a couple hours and we have no chairs."

"Well, you're in a world of hurt, Son." She pointed into the hall. "Those chairs went to Glenn and Ella Mae's fiftieth weddin' anniversary. You boys are plum out a luck."

"Well, shee-it," Kal said.

"Shush, Boy," Mabel said. "This is the house of the Lord. You best be goin' and findin' some chairs somewhere else."

"Yes, Ma'am," Kyle said. "Kal, you apologize to the Lord and these women for your gross outburst."

Kal looked up to the ceiling. "Sorry, Lord, and sorry ladies. No offense."

"None taken," Mabel said. "Now get goin'. You got some huntin' to do."

The boys ran out of the kitchen and through Fellowship Hall as they heard the Mabel return to their argument with a "Damnit, that's not right, Gertrude." When they got to the truck, they stopped dead in their tracks, looked at each other and said in unison: "Lawn chairs."

They peeled out of the parking lot, threw up rocks on the road and headed back toward their house, stopping at every farm along the way, asking for lawn chairs. In the next hour they had collected over a hundred and fifty. Farmers were well prepared for outdoor barbecues. Several said they would pitch in and bring their wagons with bales of hay for seats.

When they pulled into the drive, their mother looked out the kitchen window to see a pile of aluminum tubes and nylon patchwork strapped down with bungee cords stacked as high as the cab. Her mouth dropped open and she gasped. When she found her voice, she said, "Oh, Lord have mercy. When the city folks see this, they'll know we're hicks for sure."

"What's the matter, Mom?" Alex asked.

"Oh. Oh, nothin', Honey. Everything's just fine. Yes, fine and dandy. Now you go on upstairs and get you a shower, and here's another glass of cold water. You keep drinkin' and coolin' off. We'll have everything ready for the weddin' in a jiffy."

Chapter Eight

The bridesmaids pulled into the drive from their beauty treatment in town. Katie's older sister, Kristen, was driving, and when she saw the boys unloading lawn chairs into the side yard and a tractor and wagon putting up bales of hay behind the chairs, she quickly turned into the circular drive in front of the house. She didn't want Katie to see what looked like a hoe-down rather than a wedding. Thankfully Katie was in the back seat between Kylee and Lisa Burgess, so none of them saw what was happening. She stopped the car and hustled everyone through the front door. She called out to her mother in the kitchen to be sure Alex wasn't around to see Katie. Her mother told her that he was upstairs in the boy's bathroom taking a shower, so the coast was clear.

Once Kristen had Katie and all the girls in her bedroom, she came back downstairs to the kitchen. "What have the boys done now? Lawn chairs?" she asked.

"Don't say anything, Kristen. All the church's chairs are at Glenn and Ella Mae's Fiftieth anniversary, so the boys did the best they could do and collected all the chairs within several miles. Some of the neighbors are helpin' out and this is the best we could do. So, just go upstairs and help Katie relax. Here, take some Jack Daniels up there with you so she's happy on her weddin' day. Maybe she won't notice the hodgepodge of a set-up we're going to have."

"What about the Burgess's? They're the ones goin' to have a snit fit."

"We'll direct their limo into the front drive and give them some refreshments in the parlor. A half hour of Jack ought to smooth things out a bit."

"Yes, Momma. Good luck with *that*."

"Who needs luck when you got Dr. Daniels administerin' the medicine?"

"Right. Wait. Did Daddy find a minister?"

"He said he was. Hold on. I'll call him on the CB and find out.

Momma walked out of the kitchen wiping her hands on her apron and went to the den where she could already hear the radio chatter of neighbors on the CB.

"Horatio? Horatio!"

"Hold on boys, Momma's callin' me. Go right ahead, Momma."

"Did you get hold of a minister?"

Someone interrupted with a "I think the ol' preacher's outta town."

"Pop? Did you get hold of that minister?"

"I'll call him right now, Honey. Hey boys, I gotta sign off and call a weddin' o-fish-ee-ant. Yeah, that's what he calls himself. I don't know. Guess cause he's the guy that makes it official. Yep, talk to you later.10-4. This is *Ray-shee-O* signing off."

The radio went quiet. Karen just shook her head. "Last person to call is the most important one we need."

"Okay, Mom," Kristen said as she started upstairs.

"Kristen! Wait a minute. Could you send your sister Kylee downstairs for a minute? I need to talk to her."

"Okay, Mom."

~~~

Kristen ran back upstairs to Katie's bedroom and told Kylee Mom wanted to see her. Kylee ran down to the kitchen and asked, "What's up?"

"Honey. Now, don't tell Katie this, but I sent Alex out into the corn field to keep him busy and to pick some bushels for the reception. Well, he got dehydrated and I think he's suffered heat exhaustion."

"Really, Mom? On his wedding day?"

"I know. I know. I feel real bad about it. Now, I've sat him down, put a fan on him and gave him water to drink, but I don't know if that's going to be enough. So, could you, please, take a look at him, and if need be, get something to make sure he's okay for the weddin'?"

"Mom! Just because I'm an EMT doesn't mean I can just use county supplies to help my future brother-in-law."

"Really? If a total stranger was suffering from heat exhaustion on the side of the road, you wouldn't stop and assist? I mean, he's in this county at the moment."

"Okay, Mom. Okay. I'll go out to my car, get what I need, and take a look at Alex. If he needs my help, I already have what I need to work my magic."

"Thank you, dear. Yes, you do that; go work your magic. I sent him upstairs to your brother's room to take a shower. He should be out by now."

Kylee found Alex lying on a bed in his boxers. When she walked in, he quickly covered up and asked her what she wanted.

"Alex, Mom told me what happened and said I might be able to help you get ready for the wedding. How are you feeling?

"Whipped. Even after the shower, I still feel hot and clammy, and tired."

Kylee felt his fore head and his arms. "Don't be shy. Get those covers off right now. We've got to get your temp down. I'll go get a towel and be right back."

She went into the bathroom, grabbed a towel and a wash cloth and soaked it in cold water. She took it back to Alex and laid the towel on his chest and the wash cloth on his head. He jumped a little when she applied the cold towel, but after a minute he said it felt good.

"Okay, Alex. What I have to do next you might not like, but it has to be done." She opened a duffel bag and pulled out an IV bag with a thin hose and a long needle.

"Now, this will only hurt for a second, but we need to get some fluids in you, and fast."

"Wait, wait," Alex said. "I hate needles, and if you shove that in my arm, I'll pass out for sure."

"Oh, Alex! Come on. We've got to get you in shape for the wedding in the next hour or so. So buck up and be a man."

"No needles, Kylee. Really."

Kylee stood for a minute and then left the room. She came back with a tall glass from the bathroom.

"Okay, Alex. You can either drink this or take the needle. Which is it?"

"Give me the glass. I'll drink it."

"You sure?"

"Yes. Give it to me."

"Alright, you asked for it." Kylee opened the top of the IV bag, poured the saline electrolyte solution into the glass and handed it to Alex. He drank it down quickly.

"Wow. That tastes great," Alex said. "Give me some more."

Kylee stared at Alex with her mouth open. "Uh, okay."

She poured another glass full and handed it to Alex. He drank it down and belched.

"More," he said.

"You got it, big boy." Kylee filled the glass again and handed it to Alex.

Alex took the glass, took two swallows and stopped. He looked up with a sour face and said, "Kylee, this tastes like shit!"

She smiled down at him and grabbed the glass. "Good. You're going to be fine now, Alex. I'll go get you some cold water. Lie down and take a nap if you need to. I'll have the boys get you up in time to get dressed."

~~~

Kylee told mom she worked her magic and Alex would be fine. She headed back to Katie's room and found her sitting crossed legged on the bed crying.

"What's the matter, Honey?" Kylee asked, hoping she hadn't seen the boys unloading the lawn chairs.

"I'm just so happy, Sis. I get to have a wedding at our home and not in that big, old stone church with that stuffy old preacher." She looked up to heaven and prayed out loud, "Forgive me, Lord. Bless the old preacher and help him recover. Amen" All the girls chimed in. "Amen."

"You're going to have the most beautiful summer outdoor wedding," Kristen said. "The air is fresh after the rain, the temp has cooled off, there's not a cloud in the sky, the lawn is cut and the flower garden is beautiful."

"Thank you Kristen. Wait, wait. Since we're having it here on the farm, you know what I'd love?"

"What?" all the girls said at once.

"I want to ride up to the back of the aisle on Beauty."

"Aaaw," her sisters sang together.

"Oh!" Lisa blurted out. "Is that a...?"

Katie cut her off. "It's a horse, my horse. She's a beautiful Appaloosa with a black spot pattern. She's my baby and now I can have her be a part of my wedding." A tear rolled down both cheeks. Her sisters surrounded and hugged her. Alex's sister just sat there and stared at this show of emotion. Could someone get that attached to a large, smelly animal? A dog, maybe. But how could she know. She was never allowed to have a pet, let alone get close to one.

"We'll sneak you into the barn and have Kal saddle and hold her for you there," said Kristen. "Then he'll lead you to the back of the chairs. That way everyone will get a surprise viewing of you and Beauty before Pop walks you down the aisle."

"What about music?" Katie asked.

Her sisters looked at one another.

Kristen spoke up. "Oh, I'm sure Mom or Pop has taken care of that. What song do you want to come down the aisle to?"

Lisa, chimed in. "The Attendants were to process to Bach's *Air on the G-string* and Katherine was coming down the aisle to Clarke's *Trumpet Voluntaire* on the church's grand pipe organ. The recessional was to be Handel's *Water Music - Hornpipe*."

It was Katie and her sisters turn to stare at Lisa. Then they all broke out in laughter.

"I'm sure Alex will be volunteerin' with *his* horn pipe after seein' Katie in her strapless scoop bustier gown," Korinne said. "Not to mention her wedding night G-String."

At that, they all broke up laughing again. Lisa just smiled.

"Speakin' of dresses, let's be sure all that eatin' and drinkin' last night didn't tighten that waistline, Katie," Kristen said. "You girls help her out. I've got to talk to Mom."

As the girls grabbed Katie's hand and pulled her off the bed to the walk-in closet, Kristen ran downstairs and into the kitchen. "Mom! Did you or Pop get some music for the wedding?"

"I think the boys were going to use their guitar amplifier with an iPod."

Kristen told her mother what music Lisa said Mrs. Burgess had picked out, and they both laughed.

"Let me check with the boys," Karen said. She went to the wall phone and called Kal. When he answered she asked about the music and then nodded her head and said, "Good. Thanks."

"Pop has taken care of it. Said he had already called his cousins from Kentucky who were in town for the NASCAR race at the Speedway," Karen said.

"Cousins from Kentucky?" Kristen asked.

Yes. You know. Cousins Calvin Ray, Bobby Ray, Billy Ray and Raymond Ray. They came all the way up here from Henderson, Kentucky. You know, they call themselves *The O'River Bottom Boys*. The *O* stand for Ohio 'cause Henderson's right on the Ohio River, and bein' from Kentucky, they didn't want anybody thinkin' they was from O-hi-o, you know. They got guitars, violins, a bass, drums and amplifiers. They've won awards, but you didn't know that 'cause you don't listen to country music no more."

"Oh, yeah. Great," Kristen said with a frown, not sure if she meant it. Then thinking about it, a smile emerged. "Yeah. Live music will be way better than the boys hittin' the wrong song on their iPod. They'd have Katie comin' down the aisle to the theme from Star Wars."

"What songs was Katie expectin' comin' and goin' down the aisle?" Karen asked.

"Well Alex's sister, Lisa, said something about a trumpet volunteer, and a," she tried not to grin, "a water hornpipe."

Karen grinned. Kristen grinned and then held her hand to her mouth to hide her giggle. They both broke out laughing.

"I'll see if your cousins know some kind of volunteer trumpet, but I don't think I'll ask them to do a horny pipe," Karen said with more laughter. "With your brothers and now Alex, we got more than enough of those around here."

Just then, the sound of a truck horn played Dixie as a line of pickup trucks pulled into the driveway and up to the back door.

"Well, look here," Karen said looking out of the sink window. "Your Kentucky cousins have arrived, and behind them, the church ladies. Guess we got food and music. So, let the festivities begin."

"I'll go tell Katie."

"Wait. Here's another car. Looks like the photographer. Better get her dressed, and keep Alex upstairs while you girls get pictures taken outside."

"Okay, Momma."

Chapter Nine

Horatio walked in the back door leading his cousins and telling them where to set up on the back patio and where the electric outlets were located for their amplifiers. Kyle and Kal followed carrying two large bags of ice each asking their mom where she wanted them. Karen directed them to clean out the wash tubs from the laundry and the water barrels from the barn and fill them with the ice, then pop and beer. Afterward, they should start to get dressed, and then help Alex and his brother once the Burgesses arrived with their tuxes. The photographer would be getting the groomsmen pictures after the bridesmaids.

After the boys were upstairs and locked away from the girls, Kristen led Katie, Korinne and Kylee, and Lisa, out the front door and down to the old oak trees lining the property along the road where a small stream rippled along the south side of the house. This was not only the most scenic spot for pictures, but it was also out of sight of all the commotion of the final preparations in the back yard. People would later comment on how happy and stress free Katie looked in her wedding pictures, reminiscing on all the craziness that happened that weekend.

Once the bridal attendants were safely upstairs, the groomsmen were called down for pictures. When the photographer found out that Alex and his brother's tuxes had not yet arrived, he had all the men dress in blue jeans and white polo's. He said the barn would make a perfect backdrop and led them in a single file out the kitchen door and across the back yard. When Alex got his first glimpse of the set up for the ceremony, he stopped dead in his tracks. The groomsmen ran into him like the three stooges.

"What is it, Alex?" Benjamin asked

"Oh my God," Alex said.

"Isn't it great?" Kal chimed in. "It's like a country hoedown, and they're always lots of fun. Can't wait to hear our cousin's band, *The O'River Bottom Boys*: Calvin Ray, Bobby Ray, Billy Ray and Raymond Ray, or as we like to call him, Ray Ray. Oooh-wee, they can play."

"Great," Alex said with a whisper. He had a vision of his mother being carried off in an ambulance. The sight of this backyard as the ceremonial site of her oldest son's wedding after her church had been destroyed by a tornado might send her over the edge. As if she could read his thoughts, his cell phone rang. He pulled it out of his coat pocket and saw that it was his mom. *Oh God.*

"Hello, Mother. Yes, they're completing the arrangements as we speak. Benjamin and I are going out to the, ah, we're going to get our pictures taken. What is it? Yes, I know you have our tuxes. We're doing casual pictures by the ba...You're going to be late?" He paused and listened. He held the phone down and told Benjamin that the limo slid off the road into the ditch "No, wait. Let me get Katie's dad. I'm sure he can find someone to get you out before the limo people send a new car from Detroit. Tell the driver to forget it. I'll call Mr. Hatfield right now. Okay, Mom? No, we won't start without you. Yes. Goodbye."

He looked at the Hatfield brothers. "Guys, the limo bringing my parents hit a curve too fast, slid off the road and into the ditch. Can your dad get them out?"

"Sure can," Kyle said. "We ain't got tractors for nothin'."

~~~

Ratio Hatfield got the call from Kyle, drove back to the barn with the mower and fired up his six cylinder diesel Case IH MX 255 farm tractor. It was equipped with an enclosed air-conditioned cab, CB, satellite radio and a performance flat screen computer. As he pulled out of the barn, he waved at the groomsmen who were posing on the shaded side of the barn next to a set antique iron tractor wheels that his father used seventy-five years ago. Alex stood transfixed as the sleek looking machine flew down the drive and out on the gravel road.

When Karen saw him go out the drive, she called him on the CB. "Where in the sam hell are you goin'."

"The Burgesses limo slid off the road. Goin' to get 'em out."

"Oh," she answered, and then gave him explicit instructions as to where the driver should drop off the Burgesses once he had them out of the ditch.

Five minutes later, Ratio drove up on the stretch limo lying head first in the ditch at *Dead Man's Curve*. Unlike the smooth curves of the highway, this was a ninety degree turn at the corner of two farms. He pulled up next to the driver who was standing by an opened back door, climbed down from the cab and shook the man's hand.

"Hi, I'm Ratio, father of the bride. Heard y'all took a slide into the gutter. Everybody okay?"

"Yes, Sir. I didn't realize the road was this slick and the curve that sharp."

"Understand, Son. How's your travelers?"

Before the driver could answer, Ratio poked his head into the opened door and saw Mr. and Mrs. Burgess and two other couples drinking martinis and a little girl with a *Faygo Red Pop*. "Howdy there. Nobody hurt?"

"Why, it's you, Mr. Hatfield," Mrs. Burgess said. "This is Alex's uncle, Eugene's brother, Thomas, and his wife, Bethany. She'll be reading a scripture at the ceremony. This is their son, Jeffrey, and his wife Diane, and their little girl, Nicole. As you can see by her white dress, she's the flower girl."

"Well, hello Princess," Ratio said to the little girl.

"It's Nicole, Mister Man."

"Nice to meet you, Nicole. You just look like a princess in your beautiful white dress."

"Mommy says I look like a bride, not a princess."

"Well, I guess she's right. Parents usually are." Ratio tipped his hat to the couples.

"Shouldn't you be dressed for the wedding?" Beatrice asked.

"Yes, Ma'am. 'Bout ready to do that. Just as soon as I pull your chariot out of the drink and get you safely..."

Mr. Burgess cut in. "You're not going to use that big dirty tractor to pull out this seventy thousand dollar car, are you?"

Ratio smiled. "You mean, you don't want me to hurt your *seventy* thousand dollar car with my *hundred-fifty* thousand dollar farm tractor?"

Beatrice butted in. "Oh, please do, Mr. Hatfield. Please get us to the church, ah, I mean, the farm on time."

"Mighty happy to oblige Mrs. Burgess, I mean, it's Beatrice, right?"

"Yes, that's right."

"Well, you can just call me *Ray-shee-oh*, that's short for Horatio.

"Please, don't hurt the car anymore than it is right now," Mr. Burgess said.

"That's *Yew-jean,* right, Mr. Burgess?" Ratio asked.

"Yes. Yes, by all means call me Eu-gene, *Ray-shio*," he said with a twist to his lips like he had just eaten a sour pickle.

"Don't you worry about your car, *Yew*-gene. Have you out in a jiffy, and without another scratch." He wiped his hand on his coveralls and offered it to Beatrice. "Now if you'll step out of the car, I'll get all four wheels back down on the road."

She took Ratio's hand and stepped out of the car. As she put her second foot on the ground, her narrow heel caught her long dress and she slipped on the muddy road. She fell backward, but Ratio caught her before she hit gravel. The dress split up the side and her shapely legs were exposed.

"Oh my God. My dress. My dress."

Ratio pulled her upright and got her on her feet. "You alright, Beatrice."

She straightened her dress. "Yes, I'm alright, thanks to you Ratio."

"No, I mean, you're *all right,*" Ratio said looking down to her legs, then back up to her eyes as he wiggled his eye brows.

Beatrice blushed. "Well, thank you Ratio."

He helped the other two ladies out of the car as the men exited the other door. He directed the couples out of the way and walked back to the tractor. He climbed in the cab, fired up the diesel and turned it around so the rear dual wheels faced the front of the limo. He pulled out a long logging chain and directed the driver to feed it to him as he slid down into the ditch and crawled under the front tires of the limo. He hooked the chain to the car's frame, crawled back out and hooked the other end to a hydraulic lift on the back of the tractor. He reached into the cab, pulled up on a lever and watched as the chain became taut and raised the car out of the ditch. He climbed back into the cab, put the tractor in gear and slowly moved sideways across the road until the limo's front tires were away from the ditch and over the road. He put the tractor in park and jumped down from the cab, reversed the lift gear and slowly let down the limo until its front tires were back on the road. The three couples let out a cheer.

Ratio crawled back under the car, unhooked his chain, stored it in the tractor and bid everyone goodbye. "Gotta clean up and get my fancy clothes on. See y'all at the weddin'."

"Wait, Mr. Hatfield, I mean, Ratio," Eugene said as he pulled out his wallet. "Let me pay you for getting us out of the ditch."

Ratio waved him off. "You're family now. We just *help* family, not charge 'em. Bye now."

Ratio spoke with the driver with his wife's directions that he should drop off the Burgess family at the front door off the circular driveway. He hopped back up into the cab, revved up the diesel and took off down the road. He called his wife on the CB and gave her a heads up that the Burgesses were on their way.

Karen Hatfield took off her apron, filled an ice bucket with ice, gathered several flavors of Faygo pop, a couple of bottles of water and took them to the parlor. She walked across the hall to the living room, opened the liquor cabinet, and put together a tray of glasses and the square bottle of Jack Daniels in the center. Just then, she heard the limo pull around the circular drive at the front of the house.

The Burgesses and guests looked out of the side windows of the limo to see a renovated three story tall white Victorian house with arches, cornices, spindles, balconies, a widow's walk, and an expansive wrap-around porch trimmed in maroon. It looked like a picture post card from the last century. Karen Hatfield walked out onto the porch and waved as they disembarked from the limo. She welcome them to her home and sympathized with them about the sudden change in wedding venue and arrangements, as well as the illness of their pastor. She assured them, with her fingers crossed behind her back, that the ceremony would be a beautiful outdoor wedding on this perfect summer day. Yes, they had a minister, live music, plenty of chairs, and a home cooked meal for all of the guests. That said, she ushered them into the parlor and began administering the sweet elixir of happiness.

Chapter Ten

The limo driver delivered Alex's and Ben's tuxes to the kitchen just as the photographer finished the casual shots and had led them back to the house. The boys saw two couples setting up a flowered arch in front of the rows of lawn chairs on either side of a wide aisle. Several farmers were arranging bales of hay at the back of the chairs to add more seats, and inadvertently, cutting out any road noise for the ceremony. They stood and listened to The O'River Bottom Boys warming up to *Dueling Banjos.*

"What's that song from?" Alex asked.

"*Deliverance,*" Kal answered with a funny grin on his face.

Alex shuttered. He double checked the band to see if one of them looked demented. He found none, but he shook his head thinking, *This will truly be a redneck wedding; maybe the disaster like Katie said.* His thoughts were interrupted by an elbow from his brother.

Three cars barreled up the drive together and parked on the adjacent field across from the ceremony chairs. All of the car doors opened and out filed a dozen of the most stunning women the boys had ever seen. Kyle and Kal started negotiating with each other over which one they were going to pick up as the women walked past the front of the chairs up to the patio. The sauntered past the band, who whistled, and up to Benjamin. The leader said "Hello" in a deep voice. A man's voice.

"Danny?" Ben asked, surprised.

"Yeah, Hi Ben. I said I'd be here with my choir. We got a gig in Lansing tonight, so we came, ah, *dressed* for the occasion. Is there a problem?"

"Ah, oh, nothing. I guess I wasn't expecting a male chorus to be, well, *dressed* in dresses."

"Didn't you know? We're an all drag-queen choir. We're getting to be well known around the state.

Kyle was now shaking his head to Kal's question as to whether the girl he picked out was really a man, because he couldn't believe it. Kyle told him to think of the dress as a kilt.

"Ben!" Alex interrupted.

"Oh, I'm so sorry. Is this your brother? I should introduce myself to the lucky man. I'm Danny McLeod and this is my choir."

"Pleased to meet you," Alex said as he gave Benjamin the look that said *I-can't-believe-you-did-this-to-me*.

Kyle stepped forward with a stupid grin on his face. "Hi there. I'm Kyle and this is my brother, Kal. I'm right in assuming all of you are men, right?"

"Yes, indeed. We're all men, though some of us here like men, if you know what I mean?" Three of the men gave the boys a finger wave.

"Oh! Okay. Great to have you here. Let me introduce you to the band, who are, coincidentally, called the *O'River Bottom Boys*, and they're all *good 'ol boys*, if you know what I mean. They're our cousins from down south who are getting quite well know themselves, especially around the NASCAR crowd, and they would..."

Danny interrupted him. "Maybe you shouldn't tell them we're *boys*, you know what I mean?" he asked with a wink.

"Oh! Okay. Y'all do look like girls. Pretty, hot girls, I might add."

The choir replied, "Thank you" in very high melodic voices. They were a choir after all.

"I'll introduce you as, ahhh..."

"Introduce me as Danielle and my choir, *The Ange-Fee*."

"Right. *An-jee Fee*. What's that mean?"

It's French, Dearie. It means Angel Fairy, one of the choir members said."

"Oh! Well, how about this? I'll introduce you as Danielle and *The Angel Choir.* Will that do?"

"Yes. That will do nicely. And don't worry," Danny said looking at Alex, "we're all professionals here. We'll work out appropriate music for the wedding. So, please lead the way, Kyle."

"Oh, man. I mean, yes, Ma'am."

The men walked back across the patio to meet the band when Danny looked out on the back yard and saw all of the lawn chairs, zeroing in on the chase lounge chairs the brothers had picked out for the mothers of the bride and groom. He wagged his finger from side to side and said, "Oh, no, no. This will never do." Looking back to the Hatfields and said, "What's the matter with you boys. Were you raised in a barn?" He looked beyond them and saw the red barn. "Well, never mind."

"What's the matter?" Kal asked.

"These chairs. You can't be serious. These are way beyond tacky" Looking back to the choir, he said, "Come on, girls. We have some re-arranging to do."

The choir giggled in response, and followed Danny into the house.

~~~

Meanwhile, Kristen had gone downstairs to see how Mom was getting along with the Burgesses and found the Jack Daniels was working its magic. She tip-toed down the hall to the kitchen to go up the back stairs when she saw the choir heading into the dining room and picking up the formal chairs and carrying them outside.

She ran back to Katie's room and told everyone that apparently Alex had invited some city slicker women to the wedding. "I guess we got some competition for us country girls for the available men tonight, and they're carrying out the dining room chairs for their seats so they don't snag their mini-dresses on the..."

"It was probably Alex's brother, Ben," Katie said. "He's now the most available bachelor in Bloomfield Hills. Isn't that right, Lisa?"

"I guess."

"Well, we'll see about who's going to snag a man today," Kristen said as she pushed up her push-up bra under her maid of honor dress.

Lisa just snickered and smiled at Katie as she remembered who Ben had invited to sing. His friend Danny had a cross-dressing choir. Everyone but her clueless brothers knew that *Pronto!* in Royal Oak was a gay night club.

~~~

Guests were arriving from the city in sleek new luxury cars, and the neighbors from miles around were arriving in shiny four-door pickup trucks.

The officiant arrived and introduced himself to Alex as Reverend Ron from Pinckney and asked Alex if he had the license. Kyle asked if it was legal to sign the license before the actual wedding.

"No problem. It isn't really legal 'til the county clerk gets it, so it doesn't make much difference, before or after. Besides, afterward, everyone wants to offer congratulations and the photographer wants to take another thousand pictures."

The boys looked at each other in dismay.

"I don't have it," Alex said. He pointed to Benjamin, who got a look of a deer in headlights. Ben said, "It's still at home."

Alex shook his head. "Really, Ben? Go in the house and ask Mom and Dad if they brought it with our tuxes." Looking back at Reverend Ron, he asked, "If we have no license, does that mean the wedding can't go on."

"No, no, Alex," Reverend Ron assured Alex. "It just means you're going to have to hunt down your witnesses, have them sign it, have you and your bride sign it, and then mail it to me. Are you going out of town on your honeymoon?"

"Yes. We're flying out tomorrow evening for Hawaii. We're staying at the Westin at the Metro Airport tonight and having our families and attendants join us for brunch in the morning."

"Okay, good. Someone in your family can bring it in the morning. If you don't mind, I'll join you for brunch at the hotel and we can get all the signing done all at once, and I can still mail it in on Monday morning."

"Oh, thank you, Reverend."

"You're welcome. I'm quite used to working out the little details of the wedding day." He looked at the ceremony arrangements and saw a group of beautiful women replacing the front row lawn chairs with polished wood and white satin chairs. He smiled and said, "But I see I have help today. Beautiful."

Just then, Ratio Hatfield walked up and greeted Reverend Ron. "Thank you so much for coming out to o-ffi-shee-ate my daughter's weddin'."

"Hello, Ratio. Always glad to help out an old friend. Besides, I had kept this weekend open so I could attend the NASCAR race. The Sprint cup isn't until tomorrow, so no loss on my part. And now I get the honor of officiating Katie's wedding."

"Couldn't have a better minister than the one who prayed me through my heart surgery some years ago. Now, I'm healthy as a horse." He started braying and stomping his foot.

"Uh, Pop? Speaking of horses," Kal said. "Kristen told me that Katie wants to ride up to meet you at the back of the aisle on Beauty, rather than you walk her out the front door."

127

"Really?" Ratio asked.

"That's what Kristen said."

"That's great! Now she can have the best friend who got her through her high school years bring her to her weddin'. Just make sure she's wearin' her ridin' boots and not some slick soled heels."

"Will do, Pop."

"And you boys better be gettin' dressed. I saw the limo driver stash your tuxes in the kitchen."

"Right," Alex said. "Let's go, Ben."

Back upstairs, they helped each other with their black pin stripe tuxes and Alex's white long tails, occasionally voting on how different parts of the outfit should be done or discarded. It was unanimous that the small black studs would not replace buttons, and it was a tie vote on how the cummerbund should be worn and whether cuff links were needed. Getting the bow ties to work took a team effort led by Alex's brother, Benjamin. His veteran groomsman status was appreciated by all.

The Ceremony

Stephen M. Goodrum

Chapter Eleven

Thirty minutes before the wedding, cars and trucks were coming from both directions of the road. Neighbors were directing traffic and flagging them into parking spots in the adjacent field as efficient as at any NASCAR race or Cedar Point Park. The O'River Bottom Boys were playing romantic country tunes with the choir singing backup. Katie and the bridesmaids were touching up their makeup in her bedroom and Alex and the groomsmen were staying in the air-conditioned kitchen per the minister's instructions. "Don't want you to burn out in those black, solar panel suits," he advised. Ratio and Karen Hatfield were entertaining the Burgesses with their second round of Dr. Daniels' elixir, laughing together as the parents told stories on their soon to be married children.

At twenty minutes and counting, a farmer drove up on his tractor, next to where people were seated, pulling a flat bed wagon. He turned off the engine, stood up, pointed to multiple coolers on the wagon and ceremoniously announced: "Cold beer and water here for all." The crowd made a bee-line for the wagon as a few of the younger country gentlemen handed out orders. Looking like a country party, the band broke into Tim McGraw's *Country Boys and Girls Gettin' Down on the Farm*.

When the drinks were passed out and the song was over, the *Angel Choir* reprimanded the band and reminded them that this was a wedding, not a bar. Danny, i.e., Danielle, recommended that the choir sing two songs that the band knew: *On the Wings of a Snow White Dove* and *Amazing Grace*. Hopefully this would keep the music respectful before the bridal party entrance. Within a few minutes, the choir had everyone's rapt attention, captured by the beauty of their looks and voices.

At the end of all six stanzas and choruses of *Amazing Grace,* the groomsmen filed out of the kitchen door and walked up to the front of the chairs on the bride's side of the arbor. The band continued to play and the choir hummed softly as the parents walked from the front door to the back of the chairs. Bales of hay were stacked with white sashes and flowers, hiding the aluminum of the lawn chairs. When the Burgesses looked out over the crowd, all they saw were well dressed city and country folk smiling and nodding at them with anticipation, a few standing to take their picture.

The band switched songs and started with a solo violin and the bass used as a cello. After a short introduction, Danielle began singing *Ave Maria.* Benjamin walked up the aisle to his mother and escorted her down the aisle with Mr. Burgess following. Then, Karen Hatfield appeared at the end of the aisle awaiting her turn. On cue, Kyle and Kal walked up the aisle, stood on either side of their mother and offered their arms for her to hold. Tears rolled down her cheeks as she grabbed both of them and glided down the aisle with her two sons. There were not many dry eyes in the crowd.

The music stopped and the officiant appeared at the front underneath the arbor. Danielle finished *Ave Maria*, the violinist changed keys and played a short introduction. With the Angel choir humming behind her, Danielle began singing *I Will Always Love You*: The city residents thought she was imitating Whitney Houston; the locals knew she was singing a Dolly Parton favorite.

The bridesmaids began filing down the aisle one at a time, smiling at the two-hundred plus crowd. As everyone was turned to watch them, the minister quickly switched the groomsmen to the proper side of the arbor. The maid of honor, Katie's sister Kristen, came down last, smiling not so much because she saw so many relatives and neighbors, but because the lawn chairs had disappeared under the suits and dresses of the crowd. She was even more pleased to see the formal dining chairs in the front row for the immediate family. The country bumpkin wedding had turned into an elegant outdoor ceremony.

Last, but not least, Nicole, the six year old flower girl, walked slowly down the aisle, shocked to see so many took a handful of petals from her basket and dropped them down on the ground. When she reached the front, she looked into the basket, saw she had some left, so she turned the basket upside down and dumped a small pile of petals at the minister's feet. people, and all of them looking at her. Every few rows, she would remember what she was supposed to do and

The microphone shrieked with feedback as the Reverend Ron announced to the congregation, "Please stand!" Everyone stood reverently and turned to the bales of hay in the back in anticipation of the beautiful bride. A grandmother along the aisle who had been taking pictures of the bridesmaids, and talking loudly due to a hearing impairment, stood and in a loud voice said,

"Well, shit! Can't see nothin' now." Those close by snickered and tried to calm her.

Instead of the bride, a little boy in a black tux holding a white pillow quickly walked down the aisle and broke into a run at the end. Reverend Ron had forgotten about the Hatfields' nephew, Jacob Ray, and his *important job*. He stopped at the front, dropped the pillow, grabbed his crotch and yelled, "I gotta pee! I gotta pee right now!" His father ran out from the seats, grabbed the little boy's hand and began jogging to the house, asking, "Can you hold it?" The little boy continued to hold himself running and yelling, "I gotta pee. I gotta pee." The entire congregation began laughing.

Once everything settled down, the guitar started several notes and Danielle once again stepped to the microphone and began to sing Kelly Clarkston's first hit, *A Moment Like This.*

Suddenly to the side, the barn door flew open and an Appaloosa trotted out and down the yard with the bride on her back, her veil flowing behind her. Katie sat regally sidesaddle on Beauty who stood sixteen hands high.

Everyone stood up, grabbed their phones and cameras and tried to take a picture. At the sudden movement of so many people, Beauty reared up and whinnied. Katie quickly threw a leg over the horse's back and held on. A gasp went up from the crowd as Beauty went into a full gallop.

Alex called out, "Katie? Katie!"

Waiting at the back for his daughter, Ratio yelled, "Ride 'em cowgirl! Yee-haw!"

Beauty took off for the road, but Katie held her reigns tight and guided her to the adjacent field where the cars were parked. Trying to turn her around, Beauty took a left and ran back around toward the front of the chairs and behind the arbor.

Alex called out "Katie!" as she rode by.

She yelled, "I'm okay. Be there in a minute." Then leaning down to the horse's ear, she said, "Come on, Girl. Take me back."

Beauty began to slow down as she reached the barn, and then to a trot as Katie led her to the back of the hay bales where her father waited. "That a girl," he said as Beauty came to a stop. Ratio grabbed the horse's bridle.

Katie threw her leg back over the saddle and slid down to the ground. The crowd cheered.

The band started up again, and Danielle sang new, inspired versus:

> *It's what we've never seen before,*
> *So tell me you think this is crazy,*
> *when I tell you the bride is finally here*
> *and now, it's the moment for this,*
> *the families have waited a lifetime*
> *to see the moment for this.*

Katie proudly walked down the aisle holding onto her father's arm. She smiled at everyone as her long dress and veil, laced with flowers, shimmered on the grass. Behind her, Beauty followed, bobbing her head up and down to the music.

Unbeknownst to Katie, some of the women in the audience were whispering to one another as she passed down the aisle. Apparently Kal had picked up the saddle nearest the barn door and not Katie's. It had been used the day before in the muddy fields and had not been cleaned. A shadow imprint of the saddle was visible on Katie's back side.

The procession was interrupted by little Jacob Ray as he burst out of the kitchen back door, his business taken care of, and ran back to the front of the chairs yelling, "Wait for me! Wait for me!" He joined the groomsmen saying, "Whew. I had to go!" His dad followed apologetically and gave Jacob his white pillow with the rings attached, not knowing that he had let out another short black-clad boy.

Just as Katie and her father reached the front of the seats, out of nowhere Rufus streaked across the front of the chairs, jumped up with his paws on Alex's chest and began energetically licking his face. Alex turned his head back and forth telling Rufus to stop, pushing him down the side of his jacket and then his pants. Rufus proceeded to excitedly hump Alex's leg.

The Burgess family, seated right in front of Alex, gasped. Best man Benjamin stood dumbfounded, at a loss of what to do. As Kyle stepped around Benjamin and grabbed the dog from behind, Kristen whispered loud enough for Katie, the attendants and the front row to hear, "Stop that Rufus. That's Katie's job." Everyone, even the Burgesses, broke into muted laughter.

Once the front row had quieted, they heard Danielle finishing the song with her own words:

> *Oh, we can't believe this is happening you see,*
> *all of us will remember for a lifetime*
> *the moment for this,*
> *Ohhh, for this.*

Katie straightened her veil and wiped the tears from her cheeks. She turned to Alex, and gave him her best smile as Kristen arranged her long white flower studded gown. She had dreamed of this day for so many years, she couldn't believe it was finally here. She couldn't believe it had turned out quite like this. She knew she would shed tears at this beautiful moment in her life, but she didn't think it would be from laughing so hard that her cheeks hurt and her belly ached.

Chapter Twelve

The officiant welcomed everyone. "We're gathered here today, in this beautiful outdoor church, in the presence of God and family and friends, to celebrate the joining together of this man and this woman in marriage. So, who gives this woman to be married to this man?"

Ratio answered in a loud voice that cracked with emotion, "Her mother and I do." With tears streaming down his face, he kissed and hugged his daughter. He turned to Alex extending his hand, then grabbed him and hugged him too. He tried to say something, but he was too choked up to speak. He backed up to sit down as Katie moved forward to stand next to Alex. In the process, he stepped on Katie's veil, her head snapped back and her veil popped off. "Oh, no. I'm so sorry, Katie dear."

Just as Katie was going to say something, Beauty stepped forward, picked up the end of the veil and started chewing on the attached flowers. Ratio grabbed her reins with one hand and tried to pull the veil away with the other, but Beauty was having none of that. A short tug of war ensued.

"It's okay, Pop," Katie said. "Let her have the veil." She turned back to Alex and said, "I don't need a veil anymore."

Ratio let go of the veil and guided Beauty away from the aisle off to the side of the chairs. He handed the reins to a neighbor to lead her back to the barn, but Beauty yanked the leads away, trotting around the back of the Bridesmaids and stood behind the arbor, nibbling at the flowers. The photographer didn't miss this once-in-a-wedding opportunity and snapped a picture of the young bride and groom facing one another, the minister behind them, and above him, a horse's white and black spotted head.

Reverend Ron gave the introduction, speaking into the microphone about the importance of marriage, the sharing of values, then adlibbing that the couple should, "continue to hold hands as you're doing right now, even when things don't go just right. Remember to say, *I love you* every day, even if through gritted teeth, or through tears of sorrow, or laughter like today."

Reverend Ron then introduced Alex's aunt, Bethany Burgess, a community theater player and a First Presbyterian reader. She stood up from a front row chair and walked up to the officiant as he handed her the microphone. An ear piercing squeal emitted from the speakers as she turned to the audience to speak. After she pointed the microphone up and the noise stopped, she said she was sorry and introduced the reading.

"Our reading on this beautiful wedding day is from the Old Testament, the Wedding Song of Solomon, or *The Song of Songs,* Chapter Two." She gave everyone a little smile and said, "With a little editing on my part."

An "*Oh, Lord*" could be heard from Alex's mom.

Bethany turned to Alex and Katie and winked.

"The bride said,

I am a rose of Sharon,

a lily of the valleys.

The groom answered,

Like a lily among thorns is my darling

among the young women.

The bride answered,

Like an apple tree

among the trees of the

> *forest is my beloved*
>
> *among the young men.*
>
> *I delight to sit in his shade,*
>
> *and his fruit is sweet to my taste.*
>
> *Let him lead me to the banquet hall,*
>
> *and let his banner over me be love.*
>
> *Strengthen me with raisins,*
>
> *refresh me with apples,*
>
> *for I am faint with love."*

Bethany paused, and smiled at Katie.

> *"Look! Here he comes,*
>
> *leaping across the mountains,*
>
> *bounding over the hills.*
>
> *My beloved is like a gazelle*
>
> *or a young stag."*

Beauty stomped and gave a whinny. Everyone laughed.

Bethany looked up from her reading confused. She shrugged and went on.

> *"Look! There he stands*
>
> *behind our wall,*
>
> *gazing through the windows,*
>
> *peering through the white lattice.*

The groom answered,

> *My beloved spoke and said to me,*
> *Arise, my darling, my beautiful one,*
> *come with me."*

Bethany turned to the crowd and lowered her voice.

> *"For lo, the winter is past,*
> *the rain is over and gone;*
> *the flowers appear on the earth;*
> *the time of the singing of birds is come,*
> *and the voice of the turtle*
> *is heard in our land."*

"Play ball," Ratio said aloud, then covered his mouth. Those sitting around him nodded in recognition of Ernie Harwell's opening day quote of the Detroit Tiger's baseball.

"That's what it's all about," Bethany added. Turning back to Alex and Katie, she said, "Playing *ball!*"

"Amen," Reverend Ron said, taking the microphone away from Bethany. She smiled and sashayed back to her seat.

Alex and Katie turned back to face each other. Reverend Ron asked them to look into each other's eyes and repeat after him.

"I take you to be my spouse.

I promise to be true to you,

in good times and bad,

in sickness and in health.

I will love and honor you,

all the days of my life."

"And we have rings?" Reverend Ron asked best man Benjamin.

Benjamin looked back and then checked his pocket. Little Jacob Ray slapped Benjamin on the leg and showed him the white pillow. Ben stooped down and started untying the strings holding the rings. He couldn't undo the double knot due to Jacob's father tying them so tight so his little boy wouldn't lose them when he jogged down the aisle.

Kyle stepped around, reached under his jacket, unsnapped a leather holder and brought out his hunting knife. Somewhere from the crowd a man's voice said, *"Now that's a knife."* He leaned down and sliced the string and the rings fell to the ground. Jacob Ray got on his knees, found them and handed them to Benjamin.

"We have rings," Benjamin said as he handed them to the minister.

Reverend Ron blessed the rings, handed them to the couple, and had them repeat after him, "With this ring, I thee wed." They both slipped the rings on the third finger of the left hand across from them.

"You've put the rings on the wrong hand," Reverend Ron whispered.

Unknowingly, he said it into the microphone. Everyone in the audience laughed.

Alex and Katie both took off their rings. Alex was about to put his ring on his left hand when Katie stopped him.

"I want to put your ring on myself, the right way."

Alex gave her the ring, he put out his left hand, and she slipped it on his ring finger.

Alex took Katie's ring from her and started to put it on her right hand again. She pulled her hand back. Thinking she was playing with him, he went to grab it. She slapped his hand and said, "Not this hand. The other one."

"Hope he does better in the bedroom," Korinne said loud enough for the microphone to pick up. The crowd laughed again.

Alex slipped the ring on her left hand and wiped the sweat from his brow.

When the crowd settled down and became quiet, Reverend Ron announced, "Let us Pray."

"Dear Lord, we thank you for this beautiful day and the beauty of the love between this couple. May their love for each other continue to be as warm as this day is hot. Amen"

"Amen!" Ratio said, nudging his wife.

Alex grinned as Katie rolled her eyes.

"Ladies and gentlemen, it is my privilege, as a minister and according to the laws of the state of Michigan, to pronounce Alex and Katie husband and wife. You may kiss the bride."

Alex turned to Katie, took her into his arms and gave her a long passionate kiss. The wedding party started cheering and whistling and the crowd started clapping, then hooting and hollering. Beauty whinnied, trotted past Reverend Ron and nudged the couple. Katie and Alex parted and patted Beauty her on the head.

Reverend Ron pushed the horse back and gave the Benediction: "Whom God has brought together, let no *one* come between."

Alex and Katie laughed.

Reverend Ron had Katie get her flowers from her sister, put her arm through Alex's arm and face the congregation.

"Ladies and gentlemen, I am happy to introduce to you for the first time, Mr. and Mrs. Alexander and Katherine Burgess."

Everyone stood and exploded in applause and cheers.

The band's electric guitar gave a three note introduction, and everyone grew quiet. Danielle's angelic voice floated across the crowd with the beautiful lyrics of Shania Twain's *From this Moment.*

Alex and Katie strode down the aisle with Beauty in tow. The wedding attendants followed as couples, arm in arm.

The officiant came forward and greeted first the Hatfields, then the Burgesses, commending them saying, "Congratulations on reaching the finish line."

As the parents filed down the aisle, the Angel Choir sang loudly and proudly, "We *Are Fa-mi-ly, All my sisters and me*." The crowd joined in as they watched the parents walk out hand in hand, the Hatfields and the Burgesses smiling, talking and laughing with one another.

Stephen M. Goodrum

The Reception

Stephen M. Goodrum

Chapter Thirteen

Reverend Ron announced that the wedding party and family would meet them later at the reception. "Please take your chairs and move them into the shade under the trees surrounding the patio where hors d'oeuvres and refreshments will be served."

The metallic racket of folding, picking up and moving the aluminum lawn chairs filled the air as the crowd made a bee line for the shade, food and drinks. The choir and the band took advantage of the transition to take a bathroom break.

The Hatfields enjoyed cook-outs and putting on parties for their friends and neighbors, so when they remodeled the old Victorian they put in an extended red brick pave stone patio with a canopy of small multi-colored lights. A circle of thirty year old leafy maple trees on a manicured lawn surrounded the patio, easily providing shade for two hundred guests. A cool breeze ruffled the leaves overhead as the scent of champagne, martinis, and brochette beef, bacon and vegetables filled the air.

To accommodate large parties, the Hatfields enlarged the kitchen to the size of a modern restaurant's filled with stainless steel appliances, added a glass surrounded sun-room with a large breakfast nook overlooking the patio, as well as full sized restrooms.

When Danny announced that the choir was heading in for a potty break, the band said, "Please, ladies first." After putting down their instruments, they followed *the ladies* into the house. Cousin Calvin Ray pushed through the *Men's* door and found all stalls locked. He looked under the first door and stood straight up. He looked again for confirmation of what he saw: a pair of high heel shoes. He ran out of the bathroom which caused his cousins to run into one another like the three stooges.

"What's the matter?" Bobby Ray asked

"The choir is using the *men's* and the women's restrooms. Y'all just have to wait." As he said it, he remembered the high heels. The pointy toes were pointing in the wrong direction. He looked back at his brothers and shook his head. "I need a drink. Let's come back later, boys."

"Drinks!" they said in unison.

Danny exited the men's restroom and walked back out to the patio.

"All you ladies done?" asked one of the Rays.

"It's all yours," he answered.

Calvin stared and just shook his head.

As the band walked into the house, they held open the door for two women carrying out the wedding cake. It was a four tier sculpted white icing cake studded with jelly beans and what looked like a horse's white lead rope winding up the side. On top, someone had stuck a toy Appaloosa with the bride taped horizontal to the saddle and the groom standing by. Laughter, then applause rippled through the crowd as the cake moved into the open.

When the band and choir had gotten their drinks, they were informed by Reverend Ron that the wedding party was ready to be introduced, and with a grin, how they wanted to be introduced. He said, "Apparently Alex and Katie are ready to rumble."

Calvin huddled the band, consulted with the choir and then took the microphone to address the crowd. In a voice like the M.C. of a heavy weight fight, he announced,

"Ladies and Gentlemen, please stand and welcome our contenders for tonight's fight." In the timbre of a trumpet, the keyboardist hit the intro notes to the theme of *Rocky,* and the choir chimed in with *"Gonna fly now."*

Everyone stood and cheered as Calvin introduced a groomsman, and then a bridesmaid, shadow boxing with each other. Even the flower girl and the ring bearer got into the act.

"And now, Ladies and Gentlemen, are you ready to rumble?"

The crowd cheered and whistles.

"For the main event of the evening, please welcome, the defending champions and victors of the day, Mr. and Mrs. Alexander and Katherine Burgess."

Danny smirked into the microphone, *"Are you ready for this?"*

The guests erupted as the band blasted the *Jock Jams* theme.

Alex and Katie trotted out of the house and and into the middle of the patio wearing boxing gloves. They touched gloves, separated and began throwing air punches at one another.

"*Whoomp there it is*!" sang the choir, and Calvin announced, "Yep, the marriage has begun!"

After the cheering and laughter died down, Calvin announced that the couple would be trading in their gloves for a more dangerous weapon, the cake knife.

Alex and Katie went to cut the cake when Beauty, after hearing all the cheering, ran up behind Alex and bumped him into the top layer. Alex came up with icing and the miniature groom stuck to his forehead. Katie took her fingers and swiped the icon and the icing off his face and licked it with her tongue. Hoots and hollers went up from the crowd.

Alex took a swipe of icing off his face and smeared it on Katie's cheek, then put some in his mouth. A chant of "*food fight*" went up from the attendants. Alex and Katie obliged and took a handful of cake each and planted it on each other's mouths and chins. Katie grabbed Alex's neck, pulled him to her and planted a sloppy cake kiss on his lips, then licked the icing off his face. Alex responded with another long, passionate kiss, and licked the icing off her face.

The Ray brothers broke into Andy Griggs *"Careful Where You Kiss Me."* Alex and Katie started dancing, with everyone clapping their hands to the beat. Ben threw Alex a wet towel and he wiped the cake and icing off Katie's face and then his own. Katie's mom took the small, round top layer off the cake, took it into the kitchen, smoothed out the icing, and stuck it into the freezer for Katie's and Alex's first anniversary, a Hatfield tradition.

One of the church ladies tugged on Calvin Ray's arm. As he turned away from the microphone, she grabbed it and announced: "Speakin' of eatin'." She held up a large brass bell and said, "Dinner is serviced! Come and get it!" She rang the bell into the microphone and drowned out the music.

Reverend Ron ran up, took the microphone, silenced the bell and called out, "Ladies and Gentlemen, could we begin with the blessing."

The crowd went quiet and Reverend Ron continued. "Thank you, thank you. Now let us pray."

"O Lord of the heavens and the earth, we thank thee for the beauty of this day. We thank thee for the love of the families and friends that made this wedding and reception possible. We pray for Pastor Stewart who is recovering from his ordeal at the Presbyterian Church and for these families' disappointment in the aftermath. But today we see the ways that you work through all of us. When it seems everything can go wrong, something good can go right. Now bless this food to our bodies and bless the many hands that have prepared it, in your name. Amen."

A few "Amens" went up from the crowd, and a long "Yee-haw" as well.

Reverend Ron added, "Please form two lines on either side of the food tables, proceed in an orderly fashion, and please allow the wedding party and families to go first. Thank you."

Katie looked at the groom and said, "Decently and in order, huh Alex?"

"Amen," Alex said as he took Katie's hand and led her and the wedding party to either side of five long tables set with a buffet of country cooking fit for a farmer-king: fried chicken, roast beef, real whipped potatoes, gravy, dressing, fresh picked green beans, sweet corn on the cob, tomatoes, peppers, fresh baked bread, fruit pies, and pieces of the wedding cake.

Lisa ended up last in the attendant line when the *Angel Choir* with Danny leading the way slid in behind her. She said hello and complimented him on the singing, not letting on that she knew that *Danielle* was really Danny. He answered in a female voice and they began a running conversation as they filled their plates with food. Calvin was on the opposite side of the buffet tables listening to the *girls* talking together, wondering if he shouldn't warn the bridesmaid about his bathroom discovery.

Ben glanced back from the front of the line to see his sister talking with Danny and instinctively shook his head at her. He dropped back to introduce her to Danny before their conversation went any further, but as he started to walk their way, Alex grabbed Ben's arm and invited him to join them at their table.

Out of the corner of her eye, Lisa caught her brother's look and head shake. She thought it would be fun to keep all of the boys thinking she didn't know that she knew what they knew, and keep them from trying to let her know. She hesitated only for a moment when it occurred to her that it might not be a good idea to flirt with a guy that did makeup better than she did. Deciding that she would just have to ask for pointers, she took Danny's hand and led him to a couple of chairs on the porch where inquiring minds who wanted to know could see them clearly.

~~~

Alex and Katie sat in the middle of the wedding party and parents. As they looked out over the patio and lawn filled with their family, friends, co-workers and neighbors sitting in an assortment of lawn chairs, the sun lighting up the leaves of the trees, they laughed at how their wedding day had turned out. What were the odds that the disasters of the preceding days could have become their perfect summer outdoor wedding. It was the first of many magical moments in their married lives.

But as is often the case, magical moments only last a minute. Their reverie was interrupted by a squawk of the microphone.

"Testing, testing?" Squawk. Screech. "Hello?"

It was Alex's mother. Calvin came up to Mrs. Burgess and told her to take her hand off the top of the microphone. The screeching stopped.

"Uh oh," Alex whispered to Katie.

"Hello? Hello. I'm Beatrice Burgess, Alex's mother."

A spattering of applause filtered through the crowd. Beatrice turn from side to side in acknowledgement and her dress swished open up to her thigh where she had split it up the side. A couple of whistles came from some young men nearby. Her daily workout at the gym had paid off.

Alex eyes grew wide and his face went white. He was speechless. Katie saw his demeanor, so she whispered in his ear, "Woo-hoo. Your mom's gotten a little tipsy, and frisky."

Silence.

Beatrice smiled at the young men and gave them a wink. "Why thank you, boys. Uh, I just want to say... what a be-u-tiful prayer the Reverend gave... and that I couldn't agree more that this day has turned out to be a won...der...full..."

Beatrice swayed a little, then caught herself with the microphone stand.

"What a won-der-full day this has become."

Eugene Burgess made it up to the microphone and slipped his arm around his wife's waist and pulled her close.

"Hi Darling Husband. You're lookin' *good*. Those drinks that Ray-shee-oh gave us sure did the trick. Like he said, *That Dr. Daniels knows Jack.*"

A spattering of laughter ran through the audience.

Eugene whispered, "Okay, Honey. Let's sit down and have some dinner."

"Yes, dear. But I have one more thing... to say, and you... coming up here re-minded me... what is was. I want to thank my son... Alex, and new daughter, Ka-tee, for... saving all of us... from an up-tight service, and a..." looking directly at her husband, "a boring ass reception at your stuffed-shirt county club."

The crowd went dead silent.

A loud whinny cut through the air as Beauty stomped the ground, snorted and whinnied again. The crowd broke into laughter and applause. Eugene led his wife back to her seat as she waved and blew kisses.

Alex's jaw dropped to his chest.

"It's okay, Zander," Katie said to him. "I think your mom's having fun."

Alex found his voice. "Oh. My. God. Did you see that dress? She's *really* drunk."

"Don't worry, Honey. I'll show you some leg later, and I think *you* need another drink. Now eat and get some pink back in those cheeks. Later, we've got some dancin' to do."

"Great."

Chapter Fourteen

After the obligatory *daddy-daughter* dance to Shania Twain's *I Feel Like a Woman*, ironically sung by Danny, and the *mother-son* dance, Willie Nelson's *Momma Don't Let Your Babies Grow Up to be Cowboys,* which was pretty much Alex holding up his mother and her being proud that he would be *a banker and such*, the band and choir took a break. Everyone filed back to the bar and Alex and Katie took their seats at the main table and toasted one another with a refilled flute of champagne.

As they took a sip, a dear crashed out of the cornfield and ran at a a full gallop into the open field where the ceremony was held. Several women screamed. The dear looked up, spotted the crowd and stopped. It turned away to run, but tripped and fell to the ground. An arrow could be seen sticking out of its flank, blood running down to the ground.

A "Yeeeee-haaaaw" erupted from the cornfield. A man in gray camouflage khakis and cowboy hat with his face covered in grease paint ran out from between the stalks carrying a hunting bow.

"What the hell?" Alex said.

Katie stood up and waved. "It's Uncle Ted."

Alex stood and asked, "Who's Uncle Ted? Wait, that looks like Ted Nu..."

"Yep, *The Motor City Madman*," Katie answered.

"Are you kidding me?"

"What the buck?" Uncle Ted said as he walked up to the dead dear.

"Looks like a ten point," Ratio said as he walked out to greet his friend. "What you doin' out this way?"

"Just out huntin' in the field over yonder, got my buck and it took off through y'all's cornfield."

"But Ted, you know it's not dear season," Ratio said.

"This one of mine, *Rate*. Tagged it with a GPS chip. Got special permission from the DNR to hunt my own. Been chasin' that son-of-a-buck for over a mile or more. Hey, I thought you were in the city at a weddin'. Didn't know you was home."

"Weather changed all that. Twister took out the church," Ratio said.

Alex looked at Katie. "Your family knows Ted?"

"Well, Mom and Pop do. They go bow hunting with him every fall, and they're kinda country neighbors. He lives over in Concord, on the other side of Brooklyn."

"Right."

Ted walked over and greeted Karen Hatfield, then up to Katie and Alex. He took off his hat and gave her a big hug, then shook Alex's hand with an iron grip. "Congratulations you two, and sorry for the inter-*ruption*."

"Good to see you, Uncle Ted," Katie said.

Alex added, "Nice to meet you, Mr. Nu..."

"Yeah, Son. Look, young man. You take care of Katie Mae here, or I might have to let *you* loose on my farm and use you for *Dear* practice. Get it?" Ted slapped Alex on the back and broke out in laughter.

"Be nice, Uncle Ted," Katie said.

"Just kiddin', Katie." Ted put on his hat and looked Alex in the eye."You hunt, Son?"

"No, Sir, Mr. Nu..."

"It's *Uncle Ted* to you, now, Son. You're part of the *Co-mmunity.* So, answer my question."

"No, Sir, uh, Uncle Ted."

"Well I got somethin' here for you to get started.

Ted held up the bow and a long leather shoulder cylinder filled with arrows. "Ever seen one of these?"

"No, Sir."

"This is a *Martin Crossfire Pro Compound Bow*. Beautiful, ain't it?"

"Sure."

Ted gave Katie the carbon fiber bow with *Nitro Hybrid* cams. He gave the leather cylinder for Alex to hold as he pulled out a carbon arrow with vanes. "This is for you, *Rookie*. You carry her arrows and she'll show you where to shoot." Ted slapped Alex on the back again. "Ha, ha, ha! Guess that's true in both ways, huh big boy?" Ted laughed.

"Ha, ha, ha," Alex mimicked.

"Thank you so much, Uncle Ted," Katie interjected.

"Yeah, thanks," Alex repeated.

Katie leaned in and gave Ted a hug. She stepped back and pointed to the buffet tables. "There's plenty of home cookin' left and the ladies will heat it up for you, if you like."

"Why, thank you darlin'," Ted said. "No need to heat it up. I like it cold, just like out in the woods."

Just then there was a commotion of aluminum chairs falling and a well-dressed woman let out a scream. The crowd's heads jerked her way but no one could see what she was upset about.

"What is it? What is it?" the woman yelled as she ran toward the patio.

"Move back!" Ted commanded.

People parted as Ted marched toward the barn and stopped about fifty yards away from a large long snouted gray and white opossum bearing his teeth and screeching. Ted ran back to Katie and grabbed the compound bow.

"Come with me, Alex, and bring your arrows. Uncle Ted's goin' to show you how to protect your woman."

Ted marched back to the edge of the crowd, drew an arrow out of Alex's leather cylinder, cocked it in the bow, paused and fired. The arrow hit the opossum square in the chest and pinned it to the barn with a red spray of blood covering its coat. Some of the the crowd cheered, and others groaned in disgust.

"Yee-haw!" Ted yelled.

Alex stood silent, his jaw dropped.

Ted slapped him on the shoulder and said, "That's how it's done, Son."

Ted trotted up to the dead animal, pulled out the arrow, caught the back legs before it hit the ground and held it up, blood spilling on his pants."Gonna have some fresh grilled possum tonight, folks. Yes sir."

Alex turned pale and walked back to Katie. "Did that just happen"

"Oh, Zander. We'll be gone before that possum's done."

"Thank God."

The band returned to their instruments and invited Ted to join them. He took their offered electric guitar, talked with them for a minute, then turned to the microphone and announced, "Gonna play my new song, a free download for all my fans on my website, *I Still Believe*."

Uncle Ted turned up the volume and started his signature Motor City ultra high-energy rhythm and blues rock and roll. All the young people starting dancing on the patio, and the older folks headed for the house to escape the loud music.

All the kids loved the beat and got out on the patio dancing with each other and with the wedding attendants or the bride and groom. Alex tried to get his niece, Nicole, to dance with him, but she seemed glued to a plate repeatedly filled with an ear of corn. She told him, "This is the best corn ever, Uncle Alex, and you have the best wedding ever, Uncle Alex."

He couldn't agree more.

Lisa dancing with Danielle raised some eyebrows, her Bloomfield Hills neighbors wondering if she was a closet gay. Bruce ended up dancing with another choir member, his spa workers wondering why he was dancing with a woman since he was openly gay.

Eventually Ben got to corner Lisa and tell her that Danielle was a man. She smiled and in a whisper said, "I know, *Dummy*, but don't tell anyone else I know that I know."

"What's Mom and the relatives going to think?" he asked.

"From the look of her, I'm not sure she *can* think. But during the next slow dance, I'm going to put a big wet one on Danny's lips so all of them think I'm gay. Maybe then they'll stop trying to set me up with their boring bean counter boys."

"Oh, I get it. So, you're using Danny to cut out the match-making."

"You know how crazy things happen at weddings and everybody ends up talking about it. Well, this is my," using her fingers to make quotes, "*crazy thing*. Actually, I'm beginning to really like her, I mean, him."

"Oh, okay, Lisa. Whatever you say."

Later, the band played some slow songs and Lisa put the promised sloppy kiss on Danny/Danielle. All of the relatives and neighbors stared, and the *find-her-a-suitor* set-ups ceased.

Katie decided the mood of the reception needed a change of pace, so she had her cousins play the obligatory group participation songs: *The Shuffle*, *The Chicken Dance*, *The Macarena*, and on a more modern country note, Brooks and Dunn's *Boot Scootin Boogie*.

As the band took a break and the crowd took a rest. Alex's cousin, Jeffrey Burgess, jogged up to Alex and Katie's table out of breath. "We've have to leave."

"What?" Alex asked, seeing a panic look on Jeffrey's face. "Slow down, man. Slow down."

"We gotta go, Alex, Katie."

"But, Jeff, it's my wedding."

"Sorry, Cuz. We gotta go, right now."

"What's up?"

"Nicole's ass exploded."

"What?

"She ate four ears of corn and her ass exploded."

"Oh, poor little girl," Katie said.

"Diane thinks its divers-colitis or something like that. Nicole's never eaten real corn on the cob. We just use frozen."

"Well, no need to run off," Alex said.

"Yep, we gotta get home. Nicole made it to the bathroom, but not quite to the stall. Diane had to clean her up and it destroyed her white dress and she's upset and crying. So, we've gotta go." Jeffrey jogged off across the yard and to their car where Diane was putting Nicole in the back seat with a shawl around her to lie down.

As the sun began slipping to the horizon, Reverend Ron took the microphone and invited everyone to take their glass for a toast to the bride and groom.

"Everyone, let us toast Alex and Katie as the sun sets on their first day of marriage. May your years be filled with many sunrises and sunsets, letting not anger shadow your day, and love fill your night."

"Here, here," the guests chimed in, slinking their glasses together, sipping their drinks, and watching the sun set over the corn fields as the band played and Calvin and Danny sang *Sunrise, Sunset.*

A cool breeze came up through the yard, bringing with it the scent of the fields with a hint of manure. Some of the guests began to get up from their chairs and gather around Alex and Katie and their family to wish them goodnight.

Calvin took the cue to finish the night with a wedding tradition and announced, "It's time for all *the single ladies* to gather on the patio for the tossing of the bride's bouquet."

Young as well as older women got up from their chairs, some excitedly, others prodded by family or friends. Alex stood to the side and saw a couple of the choir *ladies* join the fray. Katie recognized Bruce from the Spa as he lined up at the back.

What happened next made it on *You Tube* in a matter of minutes and went viral on the internet from a variety of cell phone videos.

Katie stood on the patio and waved her bundle of fresh flowers. This caught the attention of Beauty, who then trotted up behind the group waiting for the toss. As the bride turned around and threw the bouquet up in the air, Beauty pushed her way into the middle of the women, knocking them to either side with her haunches and slapping Bruce away with her tail. She whinnied, reared up and caught the flowers in mid-air. The bride squealed with laughter and the startled crowd burst into a cheer: "Beau-tee, Beau-tee, Beau-tee."

To honor the horse, the Ray brothers broke into a familiar intro: *"DUM-DE-DE-DUM, DE-DE-DUM-DE-DE-DUM, DE-DAA-DAAAAA, DUM-DE-DE-DUM, DE-DE-DUM-DE-DE-DUM, DE-DAA-DAA-DAA-DAA-DAAAA.* Everyone joined the band in the chorus of Big and Rich's hit: *Save a Horse (Ride a Cowboy).*

Just as they finished the last note, everyone heard a *Yeeeee-haaaaw* coming from near the house. The smell of grilled game wafted across the patio.

"Fresh grilled possum ready for your enjoyment," Uncle Ted yelled, holding up the smoldering carcass.

"That's our cue," Alex said to Katie.

"Right behind you."

The Postlude

The Oakland Press, Oakland County, MI – Society News.

Mr. and Mrs. Eugene Burgess of Bloomfield Hills celebrated the marriage of their son, Alexander Burgess, a graduate of Michigan State University with a B.S. degree in business, to Katherine Hatfield of Norvell Twp., also a graduate of Michigan State with a B.A. degree in education.

Due to this past Thursday's tornado that ripped through Oakland County, destroying the roof of the First Presbyterian Church of Bloomfield Hills, the wedding was held at the home of Katherine's parents, Mr. and Mrs. Horatio Hatfield. The couple tied the knot in a beautiful outdoor ceremony, followed by what Mrs. Burgess described as "a down home country good time, an experience reminiscent of my western Michigan up-bringing." The Happy couple flew out from Detroit Metro airport after a family brunch at the Westin hotel. They are honeymooning in Hawaii before returning to Michigan where Alexander will become partner in his father's successful Burgess Investment Company. Katherine plans to begin teaching in the Huron Valley School District.

~~~

The Brooklyn Exponent, Brooklyn MI – Wedding News

Mr. and Mrs. Horatio Hatfield hosted the wedding of their daughter, Katherine *Katie* Hatfield, to Mr. Alexander Burgess of Oakland County this past Saturday. The Hatfields offered their *One of the Top Ten Farms in Michigan* after last Thursday's tornado took off the roof of the First Presbyterian Church of Bloomfield Hills. To say that last Thursday's disaster turned into a blessing for the couple and their families and friends would be an understatement. Thanks to the ever generous Hatfields and their neighbors, the wedding was held outdoors on what has to be one of the nicest Saturdays of the year. The NASCAR race fans appreciated it too.

Music was provided by none other than *The O'River Boys,* winner of last year's CMA award for Best Group Video. Little did the *Exponent* know that the Ray Brothers are kissing cousins to Horatio Hatfield. They gave a crowd pleasing rendition of the Star Spangled Banner at the start of the *Pure Michigan Sprint Cup 400* at the Michigan International Speedway on Sunday. Joining them was the beautiful voices and looks of *The Angel Choir,* a twelve voice choir from Royal Oak, Michigan.

A well-known local became the wedding crasher. None other than Uncle Ted from Concord. He presented the newlyweds with a compound bow and some fresh grilled opossum.

The night ended with the traditional tossing of the bride's bouquet, and what happened next became *The Brooklyn Exponent's* "Wedding Picture of the Year," None other than Katie's Appaloosa charge through the crowd and caught the flowers and promptly ate them.

What could have been a clash of cultures, the wedding and reception turned out to be a gala country event that even Mrs. Beatrice Burgess described as "a down home country good time, an experience reminiscent of my western Michigan up-bringing." Mrs. Karen Hatfield was quoted as saying, "It was more exciting than my own wedding in this very same yard some thirty years ago." Horatio Hatfield added: "I don't think anyone has seen a more dramatic entrance to a wedding that what my little girl did on her horse, Beauty." We concur.

~~~

Katie and Alex sat together holding hands in silence listening to the rolling waves of the Pacific lap up on Kauai's west's Kekaha Beach at sunset. The smell of salt water, seaweed and coconut oil mixed with sweat filled their senses after a relaxing day in and around the ocean. As the sun slipped into the ocean giving off the mythical green flash, they looked into each other's eyes and kissed.

"Isn't it beautiful, Alex?"

"Yes. As beautiful as you walking down the aisle on our wedding day."

Katie squeezed his hand and said, "Oh, *Zan-der*. You can be so romantic sometimes." She pressed her lips to his and he reciprocated.

When they finally released, Alex asked, "Speaking of our wedding day, does this mean it's time to head back to our honeymoon cottage and *horse around*?"

Katie stood up, put her hands on her hips, tilted her head and sighed.

"What?" Alex asked.

She reached down, took his hands, pulled him up and sighed. "Really?"

"What?"

179

Well, giddy up, *Buckaroo*. I guess it's time to go and *save a horse*! And, thanks to my brothers, I still know the direction."

~~~

On their first anniversary, Katie and Alex had Sunday dinner out at *The Historic Holly Hotel,* not far from their new home on Busch Lake in Holly, Michigan. They skipped dessert so they could return home and complete the family tradition of eating the preserved top layer of their wedding cake.

Katie had fished the cake out of the freezer before dinner so it would be thawed out when they returned home. She pulled their wedding cake knife out of its holder while Alex opened a bottle of champagne and grabbed two crystal flutes. They met at the dining room table and stood next to one another in front of the small round white form. They toasted one another with "Happy Anniversary," clinked their glasses together and sipped champagne.

"Okay, ready?" asked Katie, sitting down her glass.

"Ready." Alex answered as he sat down his glass. "Do you think the cake will still be any good?"

"Let's find out. Hand me the knife."

When Alex handed her the knife, she kept his hand on the handle with hers. "Let's cut it just like we did on our wedding day."

"Where's the horse with the bride hanging on?" Alex asked.

"Very funny," Katie answered. "If I remember right, the groom had a shovel."

"Did not. It was holding the reins on the front end, not the back end. So, can we just do this?"

"Alright. Here we go."

They slowly pressed the knife down in the middle of the round cake through the icing. Instead of a smooth cut, they met with resistance.

"Is it still frozen?" Alex asked.

Katie looked at Alex with exasperation. "It's been out for several hours. So, no, it's not frozen."

"Okay. Let's push down a little harder."

"Carefully," Katie said as she guided the knife.

A squeak emitted from the cake.

"Huh?" Alex said looking at Katie.

Katie started sawing with the knife: Eeeeee, eeeee, eeeee, eeeee "Oh, no."

"Oh, no, what?" Alex asked.

"The cake is fake," Katie said as she continued sawing through the cake.

"Fake?"

Katie picked up the round form, wiped off chunks of crystallized frosting and held up a soft, solid shape. "Styrofoam!"

"Are you kidding me?"

"No kidding."

"So, what are we going to do for dessert now?"

"Got something in mind?"

"As a matter of fact, I do," Alex said, wiggling his eye brows. "It's a dessert that doesn't *add* calories to your girlish figure, but actually *burns* them."

"Oooo. I think I'd like some of that dessert. And you know what?"

"What?" Alex asked as he grabbed Katie's hand and led her down the hallway to the bedroom.

"I've got an outfit *so* appropriate for burning calories."

"Really?"

"Yep. It will not only move your hips. It will make your head spin around."

"Uh oh. Not..."

"Yes sir. Just for you. Tassels."

"Really?"

"Really. Oh wait," Katie said as she stopped abruptly.

"What's wrong?"

"I think I'm going to be sick."

"Oh no. Is it the food?."

"No, I don't think so, Zander," Katie said as she ran for the bathroom.

"What could it be?"

Stephen M. Goodrum

About the Author

Stephen M. Goodrum is an ordained Presbyterian minister and a licensed social worker. He was the pastor of churches for over twenty years, and has worked for an outreach program in Detroit for the past eighteen years. He lives with his wife, Donna, and their dog and cat in Holly, Michigan. He and his wife have officiated weddings throughout Michigan for over thirty years.

He is also the author of *Blue Water Dead*, an Action Suspense Romance that evolves into an incident of national security. Set on the northern international border of Michigan and Motown, Vincent Hardesty, a wealthy undercover Homeland Security agent, must solve the mystery and expose a terrorist cell while protecting his close friends and the one woman who might end his self imposed loneliness, Graciella Venusuela Sanchez.

Contact him on his website:
www.authorstephenmgoodrum.com,
on Facebook/authorstephenmgoodrum,
and on Twitter @StephenMGoodrum